I0561783

Entertain Simpatico

Les Cook

Published by Travel Intrigue, 2024.

This is a work of fiction. Similarities to real people, places, or events are entirely coincidental.

ENTERTAIN SIMPATICO

First edition. December 9, 2024.

ISBN: 978-1738328710

Written by Les Cook.

Entertain Simpatico began in 2012. The Original, sat for years. Restructured, rewrote 2021.

A Travel Intrigue Production

Trips of the mind. For better understanding of living.

Intended for a mature audience of 18 years of age.

Some content is not suitable for persons of a limited imagination.

The story is for enjoyment and creative thinking.

Library and Archives Canada. Legal Deposit

Contact: Travelintrigue@gmail.com

lescook360@gmail.com

https://www.tiktok.com/@travelintrigue

Table of Contents

Arrival

———

IT WAS HOT OUTSIDE.

Too hot to see clearly.

Intuition... it delights; senses are sought, avoided, and yet to be learned.

I could feel her as strong as any woman I'd felt. From distance, she walked in slow silent balanced speed. Sporting a headscarf and pant-dress.

A lengthy neck. She seemed tall, slim, unique.

A gift from the spirits.

Only six hundred meters away was a canteen with cooling fans nutritious treats and refreshing drinks.

I waited for her to cross the dirt in front of me.

I walked near her, disgusted.

She wasn't ugly, just not as beautiful as she appeared from distance.

Impossible dream.

Desert Woman apparition. I thought I deserved one last pleasurable woman of the 8th and half degree. Looked like a horrifying six weeks observing construction of a wall (fence).

Extreme happy disappointment.

Be subtle; don't call names. Offense is the best defensive when you haven't anything to back it up. Defense is best to promote offense when you have nothing upfront.

Stand in the center, equal and logical. No need to attack or be attacked because you have position. Calling names is eliminated. You can move right you can move left.

I'm not going anywhere with this.

I'm just plotting while I put in my hours observing.

Welcome to Simpatico, a new type of state. Artificial Intelligence-governed design. A computer decides direction and the best human candidates to lead. A place where techno-invention and innovation are king. Products available now or soon; other products are future dream failed.

Call it a nation, call it a company. Simpatico is a State, a State of Being.

Territory was conceded: 'Go ahead, see what you can do.' Sometimes I think countries of the United Nations hope the experiment will fail, though the opposite has happened.

Simpatico calculated that democracy has trouble voting in the right leader. Let computers calculate the leader. Let AI banish, bonus, correct the leaders. No bribes no friends, the success of the program.

My observation role is to note witness report the collaboration and interaction of two entities sharing responsibility of fence construction to surround Simpatico.

Sometimes I question and listen.

Whom do I prefer, companies of Nations or Simpatico? Either, neither. If they shake hands fairly and give me no fear, I'm fine with both.

I am a citizen of a UN Country, so I can certainly criticize that.

Simpatico calls everywhere else in the world "Society" or "Earth".

I don't know anything really. Finished my last job and came here.

This place doesn't get anything full: a semi-desert, foothills, a small peaceful lake, a stream, and a center guests mostly can't visit.

Another observation day done.

I drive off the main road a half kilometer to a mostly abandoned set of travel huts to piss, ponder, and finish the day.

Simpatico placed rest stops and travel huts for pleasure, for pilgrims, nomads, and Simpatico Residents. Portable washrooms, outdoor barbecues, stoves for cooking and heat. Solar panels. Wooden tables to sleep. Simpatico ensures weekly upkeep.

Many travelers set up their own tents, use the facilities, sometimes they move from one location to another for months. They love it.

Simpatico has a heart — 'If you have traveled this far to see Simpatico, take shelter until AI decides if you are in or out.

A lot of destitute came here — hence commissioning of the huts. Travelers have since been moved out for fence construction and security.

On the other side of the road, a dark-haired man with a mustache and potbelly paces between a Simpatico truck and a hut.

After washing my hands, I think to continue, on my way.

I pause, as the mustached man enters the hut.

He re-emerges out of the hut quickly.

I walk towards my truck.

A tall skinny light-haired man shows his smiling face exiting the hut. The potbelly man waves his hand 'hurry up' at the skinny man. The men look towards me, as I'm seated in my truck looking towards them.

A woman emerges from the hut with a knapsack. Her long hair wrapped held up by a silk scarf. She appears desirable from distance.

The potbelly man annoyed, 'No ride for you' wiggling his finger towards the woman.

Displeased she drops the knapsack and picks up a rock. Threatening them.

She drops the rock as the men back away and step into the truck.

The truck begins to peel away.

She picks up a pebble and throws it, missing the truck intentionally.

Excitement vanished she walks to a water tap for washing. With a pool of water in the washing container, she cleans her face, forehead, neck, arms. She dries with a hand towel from her knapsack.

She has the same tantalizing skin as the woman I first laid eyes on the day I arrived. I can't say it is the same woman — I can't say anything for sure, as our first meeting was dream-like. This is cruel reality.

She now cleans up paper garbage blown by the wind in front of the hut. She stretches her arms, twists her neck, begins walking with her knapsack. It may be a fifteen-minute walk to the nearest transportation hub on the main road. Slightly tiresome, though easily doable.

Indeed, I will offer her a ride to where she needs to be. I drive near, park, step out of the truck. She does not turn to view me.

'Hello, excuse me,' I offer her a ride.

She asks 'Why?'

I reply, 'Why not.'

She says 'Alright.'

I say, 'Get in.'

'You want to know what that was about? You want to know?' she asks again, her eyes blazing light to my sight.

'Don't talk, just enjoy the ride. Where do I take you?'

'Heaven.'

'Oh, you believe in ancient theory, the theory that misconstrued truth.'

She thinks... then she squeezes my arm. 'Go towards South Gate,' she directs. 'I can walk in from there.'

She is a Simpatico Resident. I follow her direction. A nine-minute drive.

'Take these.' She hands me a Favor receipt. Favor receipts are the funds used in Simpatico.

'I can't,' I grumble.

'If you don't let me fund the ride, I will not let you drive me again.'

'Okay. Thank you. But I can't use it, the Favor receipt.'

'I've seen you. I know you are not Simpatico.' She ponders before resuming her speech, 'You can trade the Favor receipt in for currency at South Gate.'

'Okay, thank you.'

'Those two men, the fat man and the skinny one, wouldn't give me a ride back unless I funded them. I wouldn't fund them. They dropped me at the travel hut and took off.'

I fold the Favor receipt back into her grip. 'Why fund me?'

'Because you haven't asked for anything?'

'They asked for something?'

She looks at me as to say don't be stupid.

We are two strangers who have just met, engaged, and promised to greet in distress again. Her face is almost of a child, innocence and truth — is what I see.

I drop her (Desert woman) off at the South gate entry and return to my meeting point. I won't mention our greeting to anyone.

I'm ten minutes late past quitting time. Not such a bad thing. Cell phone service is terrible here. The closer to Simpatico the worse it gets. Contractors use radios. Simpatico has its own communication system for Residents.

Babble Skorn, Mohamed, and Maria will just have to wait. Babble Skorn is Lead Observer. Maria and Mohamed are UN contractor representatives overseeing our operation for the company paying half our wage. Simpatico pays the other half. Simpatico doesn't seem to have representation, we input our reports and send them to a Simpatico server.

We have never received feedback from Simpatico, we follow the instructions we were given initially. Simpatico is quiet, nice.

'Where have you been?' Babble asks.

'Sorry... something came up.'

Babble looks at me with understanding. 'Observation related.'

I nod.

Babble is the smartest, stupidest man I know. He can find his way out of trouble.

Why find trouble, you may ask? Because you learn.

I like working with Babble. Friends for over eight years. He said I fit the essence of Simpatico, offered me this position. Babble's personality and conversation abilities have arresting qualities. He is somewhat handsome, with a liar's charm. A slight wave of brown hair covers hefty eyebrows accenting a distinct nose. Not a big man, strong for his size when in shape. He's more than half-fit at forty-two years of age.

I catch up with Mohamed, a good-looking 29-year-old, and Maria a plain looking 31-year-old. Mohamed and Maria are both outstanding individuals; we know they have a job to do as we do. Respect both ways. Sometimes Babble and I joke they are kissing in the bluffs when they are late to meet us. Suggestive comedy like this every day.

Afterwards, we carry on towards the hotel in the nearest town where we stay nearly twenty minutes away.

Simpatico was created 7 years ago.

Inhabited by Residents 5.6 years ago.

A Vacation Resort opening soon.

2

MANY CALL IT A CULT — a modern temple.

Business is good.

Advanced Human Experimentation. Gaming Division. Seamless Safety Division or as some in Society like to say, "Mind Weapon Division". The list of Divisions is lengthy: Green Planet Division... funny, everyone likes or laughs at that one. After all, we are treading on an organic spaceship to mutate.

The town folk and others near and far populate jobs Simpatico Residents don't volunteer to do themselves.

I'm not sure if it is her (Desert Woman) because I like what I see.

I'm in the canteen. She wanders over while I stand gawking at delicacies I won't snack.

I accept a health drink. She steps to me. We don't converse, we flirt, laugh, pause in glare.

She's appealing — nice eyes with surprise. I overlook her inequalities quickly. She seems to ignore mine.

Outside the canteen I lean on a boulder, she trips near me, almost falling over.

'Sorry,' her hand clutch's my shoulder.

Her jacket is tossed on a boulder next to where I lean. She asks my name.

'Lucky Ce' is my name.

Her name is 'Absentine.'

Absentine is responsible for distribution of drinking water and other environmental aqua streams.

'What's an Observer do?' she asks in glowing respect.

In comedic straight face, 'I construct verse for short stories I write.'

She nearly laughs before upping me, 'I was accepted to Simpatico because I told them I have an abundance of invisible energy.'

'Genius,' I stroke her voice.

Popular religion and prayer are not practiced in Simpatico. Meditation is preferred.

Absentine moves forward, 'I wrote one sentence: "I have an abundance of positive energy".'

I nod in agreement.

Absentine looks down then up clear to my eyes, 'You have an abundance of spare energy. Sunshine smiling.' She laughs.

I smirk back. Go ahead, check me out. I swear to myself.

Her eyes dilate sure as she speaks, 'Simpatico liked what I claimed, granted me residency.'

From this day on she says she'll pay special attention in the areas I observe. A Simpatico Resident must perform a task. They all must Serve Simpatico in some capacity. Absentine volunteered to serve full-time now and part-time later. Someone must do the water job, and she thought why not, maybe fun. 'When I tire of it... I'll find something else.'

When Babble first mentioned the opportunity to work as an Observer, I said to him, 'Isn't Simpatico followed like a cult?'

'More than a cult,' he answered, 'the most advanced building blocks on Earth.'

I tested his knowledge. 'What kind of people go live there?'

'A genius that needs funding, an outlaw inventor, a person who has nothing, a person who has everything though remains empty.'

I began to read hate info and unbelievable positive information on Simpatico. Curved truths. Hyperbolic belittlement. Tantalizing encouragement.

Must go see to believe.

A place of brainwash, the hate.

The ability to mind read, the love.

The Worst: Serve a corporation for minimum wage. Worse than socialism. Secret police. Inhuman.

The Best: Be one with technology, your natural self is unleashed to an advanced creative state.

I think: Human made loves machines. Democracy would vote for technology. A dictator would use technology. A communist change their mind, adapt or fail. Would a computer system approve? Yes.

Babble likes to say, 'What about hacks? Won't someone hack Simpatico?'

I always answer 'I don't know' because Babble and I don't know. I manage my working days with imagination, conversation, walking, and write verse.

Get paid to write a novel is what I like to say. Daily entertainment with Babble Skorn, laughter and arguing rules the days.

I quit my last job and came straight here. I didn't even have time to go home and see my family.

Displeased lonely excited. A new adventure, money, a unique place. Happy to please, easily annoyed. I've been away from home over six months. Six months is long enough to start to forget about your family and home. Three months is when loneliness and weakness set in, you aren't hardened. Five months away you begin to forget home, thinking of the life you're living and what could be. Maybe I wanted to forget home as I accepted this job. No vacation from one job to another because this job is a one-of-kind special event. My family agrees there will be plenty of family time later.

After being away from home this long... I'm open for offers.

'Watch out for that one' Babble nods towards Absentine smiling ecstatic, a statue living screaming "Hot Woman" upright determined in charge. Stunning.

I find my attraction to Absentine peculiar... I'm trying to secure my feelings true and my eyesight false. Babble gives me permission with caution — proceed but don't complain later. He can feel her allure too — except he is one to think he's to fuck her once if chance arises and nothing more.

Absentine certainly is unique, mildly excepting. She may not have the appearance of a heavenly adoring sensual gift, though she may well be just as endearing. How quick things change. The past can feel the future and the future can reshape the past.

Maybe I'm not to have one grand affair. Beating in the blood, pounding in the heart, deep in the brain I don't care — only in the artificial mind with my animal cock I care.

Do I really want to fuck? Course I do.

Do I have the mindset to have a full-on affair? Overthink it later when they decide what they want from you. Now, be an animal. It is true as they say, play, fornicate, walk away, dream, laugh, write, tell stories of it. Everyone is always in love, real or not, your mind doesn't care.

I have never voted in my democratic home country, no accountability for the nation's failures nor its success. Voting is to believe in the system. By not voting, I have voted.

I survive.

Simpatico: A bright idea of one person, backed by many. A manifesto was designed executed. The Simpatico inventor has never been heard from again. Teams of followers analyze, document, advise. A computer interface called "Portal" directs.

Scoff, shake your head.

The Simpatico spokesperson says, 'The proof is in the pudding.'

The Simpatico selected Governor says, 'History is private. If you don't believe don't invest, don't apply for residency, do not contract as specialist, guest, visitor, do not sample as vacationer or tourist.'

Simpatico is working to stamp out conspiracy. For the Resident none of it resembles the former space they resided no matter what country they came from. Doesn't matter if you came from South America, Australia, Africa, you are from Earth Society.

Simpatico considers itself nothing like the rest of world.

I'm here to observe the tandem effort to construct a fence that separates the lawless, the blinded, the wildlife, the perceived free, and the advanced. A wall protecting inventiveness, or is the wall protecting the rest of the world?

Is the wall to keep them in, or keep them out? I haven't considered which is most dangerous, desperate. After all, I've only parked at the entrance.

An airport is part of Simpatico territory seven kilometers east of the fence. The roadway to the airport is considered Simpatico territory. Seamless security is in place. International Residents,

Guests, and Specialist cannot venture outside Simpatico territory unless they have the proper paperwork.

Absentine is an International Resident with a temporary day pass to serve fence construction.

Simpatico technically advanced security is secret knowledge. I've seen robots, drones, remote vehicles, motion detectors, cameras, but no dogs.

Illegals in Simpatico is a thing "Alternative world" distributed underground around the globe. If you can get in you can stay in as a "Bandit". Problem is you may never have permission to leave and enter again. (If you had permission to enter Simpatico temporarily, but never left; you become a Bandit)

Travelers that enter Simpatico without permission are found, escorted out-of-bounds, no more travel hut for them, and no possibility of future permission to return and enter.

Everybody in Simpatico has been identified.

Simpatico calculated... build a wall. They needed a fence to satisfy its neighbor. Tired of calls of wandering strangers. Community is essential, as is to be an individual. Society suggested a fence in the beginning but no, this was supposed to be the free world.

Society conceded land in exchange for the extra security of a fence. This exchange was Babble's in to Observe as Society wanted eyes, supplied material and construction teams.

You always want freedom. The bad also come in. Protection needed. Rules established.

Babble likes to dream he was selected by Simpatico; in reality, he knew a guy.

Babble provided a presentation on Neutral Observing. His contact submitted the idea to Simpatico first. Second his contact submitted the idea to a United Nations contractor. UN contractor went to Simpatico for approval. Simpatico already knowing Babble's plan agreed to let him be an Observer, playing it safe granting limited access.

Babble played them both. Our reports all positive to both sides plus a little encouraging negativity.

Babble and I were given the Simpatico Visitor and Guest pamphlets, tourist information, vision, plus Resident application to read. We haven't filled out the Resident application form. We could apply as Specialist, though we do not have a quality needed. A work pass was granted noting we are friendly though no approval to be inside Simpatico.

Absentine rests near me, 'Do you remember those men in the hut with me?'

I do.

'They would have tried to rape me if you were not nearby. They saw you. I didn't want to tell you everything. The fat one playing with himself in front of me. I just laughed "Get away". The tall skinny one trying to console me, I rifled "Get lost". Really though I was scared.' Her eyes set. 'If you hadn't shown up, I don't know what would have happened. You never asked about it. And that's what I like about you. I've thought you must wonder?'

'I wondered why you were out there on the road; I thought restroom.'

'Oh. Not why in the first place?'

'Yes, why in the first place?'

'I don't know... I don't know why I was with them. Maybe I was leading them on, I don't know. They offered me a ride to Simpatico. Quicker than taking the transport van.'

'And it turned out longer.'

'There are no short-cuts. Right?'

I agree.

'You should know, I have not been with any man for a very long time, years.' She smiles, her face flushed with happiness.

She travels in the transport van daily to and from Simpatico.

I leave Absentine.

A Simpatico woman walks close to me, she's viewed our conversation. The woman confronts me, 'When you are nice and help a Simpatico woman, she'll love you forever.'

3

ABSENTINE COMES AROUND slow and sometimes quick. When I speak, her ears peak.

We wave from distance, smiles galore. She claims she likes women too, with her finger to her lips 'Quiet, don't tell anyone.'

I don't dare or care because I know she likes me. No competition — a perfect companion.

She asks my story. I tell of my marriage. My wickedly smart beautifully charmed life.

Absentine comes to me for fun, advice. She is loudest to laugh when I joke, first to debate when I contemplate.

Broken damaged skilled, devil bizarre, she asks if she can make me breakfast and bring it to site.

I say, 'No. The hotel provides.'

I'm stupid I should have tried her meals see what she tastes like.

In two days, I ask her if she's a good cook.

She laughs 'Yes.' She thinks about the question and says, 'Ce, stay out of my head.' Good I'm in her head. When will she be on mine?

Cooking straight to the heart.

She brings me lunch she's made, tastes delicious I can live with her. Maybe I'm off-track thinking Absentine. Other men haven't talked of her in alluring ways, only rudeness, work, and water. All I see is her smile. I think she hides her tight body, her glorious thin bones — a knockout that goes unnoticed. I notice.

I heard a construction man complain, 'No, not her; there's another nice water girl from Simpatico.' I couldn't see why the complaint — I was happy to see her and not the other girl who may have a pretty face and pleasant ways — but I'd rather swirl my mind in Absentine.

Am I the only one with clear sight?

I do see some folks friendly with her. I see she has mates. Like all humans she is somewhat liked and a little misunderstood.

Her clothing reprehensible, awful, laughable. She doesn't wear makeup and when she does, it looks like it's from a teenage shop. That's a good thing —she doesn't need makeup. Her face has an awkward enticing shape, eyes large dynamic, skin acceptable, frame in shape. I can't figure out if she's lovely or fair.

Babble likes to say, 'She doesn't know what she is — African, Arabic, Asian, European, her wavy hair, her sometimes light skin tone, her sometimes dark skin tone.'

But she'll tell you she knows exactly whom she is —a Simpatico Resident.

If you have nothing else, you come.

Can't stand society any longer you come.

Have all the money in the world want something new, you come.

If you are sly, if you are lucky, you come.

I keep sensing Absentine at distance.

I say time distance money will join on a collision for us.

She tells me about spiritual love about spiritual intimacy 'Have you done it?' She insists I must.

'I don't know.' I shrug her off.

She goes directly to my eyes, 'This can be done when the right spirit is rung. In agreement in the same dimensional degree.' She laughs teasingly, blushing, stroking my arm then my chest, before flaunting away.

I grasp her arm pull her back towards me. She won't look up. Bites my shoulder with wet lips.

Absentine drenched in my guise.

I'm a Greek God.

I pull her up to my eyes, she pulls mine down to hers. 'You want me to break in... or break you out?'

She laughs. 'You are married Ce, stay away from me.'

Spiritual genius.

I laugh.

'Who are you?' I ask.

She knows exactly where her ex-husband is — dead to her life. Divorced. She has a ten-year-old child that stays with her.

I pulled another woman close near on the road and I thought Absentine was about to cry, she stormed off not saying goodbye.

It felt like being hit by a plank of wood. I knew Absentine liked me. Hell, now I realize it, shouting out loud.

Maybe I am interested.

Shall it matter if she is my devil present of this universe?

Should I go to the bank buy her away from here? I don't have enough money, a good thing. She hasn't documentation to wander around town. Why don't I just meet Absentine at a travel hut? Neither one of us would be wrong. I don't know or understand all the details of Simpatico culture.

Does Absentine hold back or not?

We can't walk together in the bush of the bluffs. We have reputation and we have positions. Out of sight, I could pick her up and drop her off. True lovers might take this chance. We are not lovers.

Perfect. Nothing may ever be fulfilled.

Simpatico is an enigma.

Babble and I are lost in an empty space of conundrum. We follow our own instructions, observe the interactions of Simpatico Residents and the non-resident service companies. We speak with non-residents who enter Simpatico daily. Truck drivers report they drop off pick up equipment and supplies, say hi and goodbye. They report nothing unusual. The same rules follow in Simpatico as with correspondence to their regular jobs. We talk to non-residents who work and sleep in Simpatico territory. They say Simpatico is unusual, they haven't a free pass to explore. They do their job and then back to their living quarters.

What does the rest of the world possess as good compared to Simpatico? They both provide you with borders.

A Resident can come and go as they please, but they do not leave unless they seek permission and have the correct paperwork. Some Residents work in the outside world setting up Simpatico designs while others command huge funds for their skills and knowledge. A Resident is free, but the answer to what they do with this freedom has consequences. An unknown path you don't know what might jump out or where it will end. Life!

The outcries from Earth: 'AI can't rule.' Simpatico says yes it can, another AI keeps the system in check.

Residents can pursue a leisure hobby, education, or training they like. If it can't be done in Simpatico or the surrounding area you can leave, pursue your passion and return. Simpatico brings in as much education, training as it possible can. What it can't bring in, it sends Residents and Specialist out to achieve.

4

—————

AT FIRST, I REFUSED to listen refused to admit I found Absentine attractive. Now after four weeks I'm beginning to think of her more than what I'd actually act upon.

My delight? My inspiration? No, she isn't as shattering as I dream. An unplaceable Simpatico woman, she belongs to something somewhere else; she is as alone as any person I've known.

We greet in exaggerated stare, studying where is my mind with a devil princess as this. She is no earthly possession, no desert queen, no utopian gem. Absentine, you are novel unique.

She takes her hand from her mind and directs it at me, pointing out that the sky is our meeting place.

Our minds connect invisibly. She doesn't have to speak; I can read her thoughts. She can't believe our transcending transcendental meetings together or apart. We sense each other as two mystics greeting. Telepathy must have a meaning or is it merely two people thinking amazing lust at the exact same time.

Any great thinker or scientist today who can prove my mind wrong, come on now, two minds — hers and mine — believe.

Her hand on my thigh, a tender squeeze. We sit on a table in the shade. We hold hands briefly before she gets up to leave.

Insistent, Absentine turned me on to the Simpatico messaging app. Gave me her contact info.

Fine.

Can it even be real, the messages, perhaps all a machine perhaps a game from my co-workers, the contractors, the Simpatico computer.

At first, our messages were of "How's it going?" or "Where are you?". Soon, our messages are funny and flirting.

Now I'm sculpting, crafting, enjoyable, worst, thrilling, punishing words.

Absentine's message: 'When I see a message from you, I smile. I can't feel good every day. You help me with that good feeling. I'm happy. You are one in a million.'

My message: 'One month in, I have so much to listen and maybe as much to tell, I'm sensitive to you. I'm true. You think this is one time. You think this is infatuation, you think this is fool, no. This is visibly invisible. Two powers striking as one. Slowly I'm rising in flight with you. Laugh at me go ahead, I say not to you but all others if they knew. Nobody knows you and I as they would cry stupidity when they look to the stars and find us shining in their eyes.'

Rebel.

Absentine picked up a cereal box and threw it against the wall of the canteen, cursing, 'Sugar'. She scowled at processed meat and loudly complained of unhealthy products this canteen offers.

The manager of the canteen asked Absentine to leave.

'Good' Absentine said, clearly pleased. 'It serves Earth's best hell. Eat this and die stupid. Where is Mother Nature?'

Absentine dropped processed meat to the floor and swore. 'Not good enough. It is unacceptable for me to eat this.' The manager called security. This canteen serves both Simpatico Residents and non-residents alike.

My gift from the universe seemed dashed. Embarrassed, I question is this really my gift?

I defy — I cannot be with her.

Self-conscious I desire her. A woman as destructive as confrontational as crude, and yet I know it is a lie. Where can I hide, and still, continue with her? It will only take a few days, and I like her even more.

A Simpatico representative came and settled the conflict. Babble attended.

Resolved, the canteen unable to secure their standard order, must still supply the contractors that are non-residents. Thus, the canteen must continue providing food service even if it does not meet Simpatico canteen standards. A shared canteen outside Simpatico territory can only follow its corporate rules and instead paid a fine for not meeting Simpatico standards. Absentine understood but did not apologize.

Absentine's statement: 'Have nothing, no food? "Go hungry" — that's what you should speak.'

She should have made her lunch at home or picked it up from a Simpatico canteen instead of relying on the unreliable one. I think she was just making a point as she never depended on this canteen.

Absentine continued: 'There is no second choice; "Fast" is the second choice if the ground, if the wind, if the spirits have decided not to deliver natural wholesome energy. Today the message is clear "Go hungry" give the stomach a break. A "Great test" and you didn't see it. A chance to help all the people be healthy with a few days of less food and the returns would be a longer more enjoyable life. Canteen, you failed.'

Babble thought Absentine was ridiculous but totally correct. She cost that company. She also cost her reputation. Nobody won. The natural order reestablished.

Babble changed his perspective as he completed his investigation: It was not the first time the canteen did not live up to its obligations, it happened consecutively for weeks.

Bravo Absentine!

Her scheme puzzling to many; a little freedom from Simpatico health food taken away.

I have seen many Simpatico Residents and Specialists enjoy processed sandwiches, sugary drinks, and even carry around a cereal box as a snack. Some Residents and Specialists used this canteen as a break from Simpatico's health-conscious cycle. Simpatico does allow for some indulgent treats, though this canteen was getting out of hand — worse than it should be.

In the end, Absentine agreed to follow correct channels to argue a program or opinion.

I wonder: where can I find a woman like this, where everything wrong seems right?

We walk together. She places her head on my shoulder in full regal unlimited submission.

No matter what someone says, I'm not shy. I'm in a kingdom. She is light firm. It will be a tidal wave when we entwine; shells of shipwrecks will be left behind.

My arms around her waist. Her neck extends. Her lips almost graze my neck.

Fellow workers are nearby.

At this moment, she is the most beautiful feeling in this detached world. Our faces glow together, her skin brushes against mine, tender, tantalizing. Romantic unison absorbs each other in body warmth. We break away slowly; we are not apart, only physically.

Internally we hold the feeling as we slowly embrace once more before saying good-bye at the exact same time. Either of us pushes away. Natural in-tuned bodies separate. The interaction last only a minute; it is enough.

As high as angels, and then crashing down with Absentine destroying processed food in the canteen. I laugh… she was right.

I stall near her quietly, 'Absentine, let's go out. Meet up.'

She obliterates me. 'No, I can't see you.'

Yet our legs touch, our eyes magnetize.

"No!" That's all right, say it a thousand times.

I'm not exhausted. Love they say is exhausting selfish, again I'm none of that.

Love is merely fuel for spirits to travel.

You think I can explain this, love is for the animal-human machine.

Humans are merging with machines; you and I are merging with invisible.

We already know we are passed merging machines.

The bright human who brags they are a star thinking they are inventors creating molding the human and machine together are thousands of years behind. I laugh. Humans must build again what is already built to understand it.

I feel you without a machine or technology.

My hands chained

I float in a capsule

I cannot see her.

I cannot see my wife.

A fatal love. A love I can't stand. A love I can't have. I am human.

AI would not do this.

A virus would.

Penalty.

Truth never revealed. Illusion never expelled.

Inoculate.

My life has become brilliant since I've begun communicating with Absentine. I feel strong, healthy. Sleeping well. I can accomplish anything. In fact, I like this job. I'm having happy correspondence with my family. My wife positive. And still, I can destroy everything and pursue Absentine. It would mean less money, a new job to support two families and on and on. But wait... in Simpatico I don't need money to love a woman, do I?

The disguise: felt so good, let everything else go.

I'm not looking to destroy anything with Absentine, she will be included.

5

———

THE SOLAR SYSTEM ISN'T perfect, though it connects to create the energy for the planet we live on.

I've deleted most of what I wrote today — most of my truth.

This morning, I was trembling in passionate intensity. Some may say the devil is draining my passion, if that were true, have me, but it isn't true.

You refill my passion instantly.

I can't even compliment your messages; you have complemented mine first.

You send considerate messages that say I'm not to be harmed. Every molecule is reading your name. Many would think I'm crazy to write the words I do of you for you to you. I'll take this chance to find our image in the sky. We both know from experience that the taste is to be exquisite.

If you don't like it or don't believe me, rip it up, burn it, and I'll keep walking alone on cold frost and the heat of clay.

Today, waiting for Babble Skorn.

When Babble returns, he knows the truth: we have limited time to visit Simpatico. We haven't procured a contract to work in Simpatico as we'd wished. It is "take chance" time.

With less than a week left, it doesn't matter we have done a good job and can act with discretion, test limits. Conversation about life in Simpatico is off limits as requested to us before we began. For the most part, we've followed protocol. "Off limits" means direct questions; casual conversation is expected.

Simpatico has Simulation Studios for the faithful, eccentric, elite, futurists, and those who enjoy games.

Three dimensions: the citizens of countries, the Resident of Simpatico, and the mystery of Simulation Studio. I'm not sure if it is a place of bright minds — it's too early to tell. Everything I say about Simpatico is theory.

'Absentine!' we yell. 'Will you please come here.'

Absentine curiously cautious, 'What's up guys?'

'Tell us about Studio. What is a Simpatico Simulation Studio?'

'I don't live in a Simpatico Studio. They are not called Simulation Studio. Just Studio. Simulation is a featured theme if that's what you are into. We have a Simulation Division. You can view, read, listen to your simulation if you have access.'

'Ok, thanks. What does "Advance in Studio" mean?'

'Even if I knew I can't tell you Earthlings.' She almost laughs. 'You see that Simpatico Information man?' points to a Simpatico Information man. 'He's a "Heavy" — he'll smash us with a hammer telling us what's right. You want me to get beat up?'

'No, no, we don't want that.'

She laughs 'Studio is where everything happens. Studio can be anything: an invention, a controlled experiment, a think tank, a simulation like the two of you think.'

'Okay, again what is Simpatico Studio?'

She laughs, 'You guys won't stop. Request a tour, an experience, or pay for a holiday vacation. Man up! Apply for residency.'

'Please Absentine tells us more.'

'You have two lives, technical and natural. Think of how, if your dream becomes alive. Think of what you dread, what you hope, what you conspire, what you fear becomes real — that is Studio. Life is up to you. What dimension you want to exist in. Step in a capsule, a helmet on your head, a drug in your system, electric against your skin, a techno-chip connected to your being, sound waves to your brain, and live in what you've created, or what someone else created. God, gods, simulation, random, human, make believe, or as real as can be. Game.' Absentine smiles, 'Shoot I don't know... as far as the mind can create, that is Studio. Studio, exactly what the word says.' I have never heard Absentine pronounce such words, sung in such verse.

Absentine walks away.

'What the fuck does that mean? We know less than we guessed,' Babble almost screams.

Riddles every time, we've asked Absentine and other Residents this question many times, and the answer is ever evolving muddle in our brains, discontent in our minds, and utter thirsting in our souls.

What they claim is vacant: meditation, psychedelics, electric pulse, laser — all of these and more. The unknown.

Let's go talk to this "Heavy".

'Do we call him Heavy?'

'No, that's slang.'

'Call him Mr. Simpatico Information Man.'

We ask the Simpatico Information Man, what Simpatico Studio is like?

He shakes his head politely, 'Whatever you like it to be.'

He is nice and considerate, not a "Heavy". Absentine fooled us.

He expands, 'It doesn't simulate life; it stimulates life. It really isn't what everyone thinks.'

'What does everyone think?'

'Everyone thinks it is a simulated life created by a human and executed through a machine.'

'So, what is it really?'

'Read the pamphlet,' he says firmly.

We read the pamphlet: The human, the cosmos, and the unknown come alive together — simpatico.

'Sounds reasonable enough.'

'The Information Man laughs. 'It is easily explainable in words, but not easy to explain in experience, mechanics, physics, philosophy, or know how. That is the trick of Simpatico, unexplainable even when explained. The explanation is one of what the user wants to believe, and the listener wants to think. Because even if it was revealed, you would not understand.'

'A riddle, like God?' Babble jabs.

'If that is the ingredient you choose,' the man concludes.

Babble guesses, 'So, you go to a library and choose which theme you like?'

'Sometimes. Or it can come from your own thoughts, and the thoughts of another you're connected to.'

'Oh, my god. You capture the thoughts of others and theirs yours at the same time?' Babble rejoices.

A shrug a nod a smile from him. 'All Residents have tried Studio. Don't let them fool you. They like to keep Studio experience to themselves.'

'So, you can explain it to us, what happened, what it is like?' We compliment in tandem.

'It's really fascinating....'

'Come on what happens?' we prod.

'Nothing really. It isn't dangerous or anything. You must try... soon, in a few days you can pay for a Vacation Studio experience. I cannot explain every theme, every experience is different.'

We nod in understanding.

'I learned this type of technology in school.' He goes on satisfied in our agreement.

'What type of school?'

'A school for creating advanced life. It is how I became a Simpatico Resident. I was studying what they have designed. Simpatico paid for my education and continues to pay for my studies. I must only Serve as an Information Officer for them when I'm not learning. Soon I will train and study here in Advanced Experimentation.'

We both agree it's great to trade serving for learning.

'Was it real?' back to the subject of Studio experience.

'As real as this,' he smiles.

'Can we do this?'

'You can apply.'

'How, where?'

'Ask Portal.'

'What is Portal?'

'Portal is the communication interface with Simpatico.'

'Security will allow us to access the Portal?'

'Yes.' The Information Man points towards the entrance a kilometer away 'A Portal is there just inside the entrance. Perhaps present a proposal to Portal to observe life inside Simpatico.'

'You think we have a chance?'

'Just like the rest of the world you can apply for many things but to be invited for an interview and accepted afterwards is always the question.'

Our proposal. We study for the rest of day and memorize our lines. We think, conspire, argue out loud during dinner at the hotel restaurant in town.

'This could be the inspiration for your science fiction novel,' Babble projects.

'I don't write science fiction, just how I see the world.'

'Ok, well your vision of the world maybe just about to change.'

'I've been interested in alternative life. It isn't a hobby it is a thought process more than imagination.'

'What else are you interested in?' Babble interrupts.

'Same as any man.'

'Like her.' Babble directs my attention to my phone.

Absentine has sent a message. Babble knows the tone of Absentine's message.

'She'd be a good one to write about,' he insists.

I agree.

'I've been having trouble writing,' I confess.

'Writer's block,' Babble comments.

'No writer's block; I don't know what that means. Passion is what I'm missing. I can't write what I think. Complaining and criticizing mostly, I need to articulate it without being vilified.'

'By the time you write your "next story" it will have been done.'

'Damn, you're smart,' I reply sarcastically.

'I know where you are coming from and where you're going. I agree, but maybe it takes someone extremely smart to write it out.'

'Is that why I can't write it?'

'No, it would take a lot of thought. Maybe you aren't up to it at this current time. You think about it because you have time to think it through, you haven't time to plot it. To you, it just sounds complaining, correcting, criticizing, and commenting.' He pauses 'I listen to what you say every day. I know you have answers, you just need to do the work and take the criticism.'

'If the work is good there will be no criticism only understanding, this is what I'm after. Writing a story is annoying. Making stuff up that doesn't exist, it's both hilarious and disgusting creating a world from nothing and saying it works.'

We end the night. Tomorrow we'll present our idea for Portal for review.

I begin to type a message to Absentine. I don't send the message. Instead, I delete the message. Save it in my notebook.

I've been struck. When will I admit it? Words help to strike it out.

6

I'M NOT A PERFECT MAN. I can make a mistake. A handcuffed man, a trapped man, an unforgiving man, a man not attending to his own needs.

People want to misbehave and spend a lot of time figuring out how to misbehave without getting caught. The foolish act outright. The clever orchestrate a sophisticated production even if discovered, can't be proven. Others never attend to their needs; they simply dream. For the successful, no grand production is needed — realization becomes reality.

Simpatico is a computer-designed society. The computer decides. I don't know how the design works. There are exceptional people in the world who've figured it out, though not the random changes. Trust Simpatico. Become part of history to advance human life. Or maybe just belong to a cult or an experiment gone wrong or gone right. People of the same mindset. A future for your children. Join have faith give up Society the other part of this distinguished world.

If you believe the Simpatico program you can stay, go, and come again. Like any society you can be expelled. As everything, all the information isn't in the pamphlet. We debate our Observer role to be in Simpatico and how to present it.

'Isn't that kind of like a reporter? I don't want to be a reporter,' I claim.

'No reporter — more propaganda or spy depending on the venture we go and how we are treated.' Babble trusts I'll agree to this explanation.

'Is propaganda, spying, conspiring, better than reporter?'

'None of it is good if it's used for the wrong means.'

We agree reporting is commendable if the reporting is sensible.

'I wouldn't use my wages to visit Studio,' I comment in humor.

Babble laughs, 'Neither would I. Screw it... let's do this adventure,' loud in allure.

We present our quest to the Portal Booth to be independent Observers.

A few hours later we return to Portal.

Portal responds: 'If you are approved no one shall know. Reservation and project will be cancelled if knowledge is known. Pay for your own travel here from your home. You will answer to Portal solely. We will take care of your accommodations, instructions, and funding rate. Come back in two days for more information.'

Two days pass.

Babble goes alone to Portal.

Clarity.

Absentine approaches the truck, passenger side window to be exact. She wants something, maybe a little bit of me.

Understanding my days are done, Absentine sighs envisioning the future, 'It will be a long time coming to find someone.' She hints I can apply for Simpatico residency. I could come as a guest, or she can leave on a holiday. She looks at me, waiting for me to choose. All her words are uncertain. All titillation, opaque conversation and thoughts to survive the day.

'You won't Serve in Simpatico... ever?' she asks.

Mind reader, I knew it.

I step out of the truck.

We cannot consume each other. I take her in my arms polite. Her eyes wide, testing — eyes of seduction, submission, lust, love, and game. Which of these eyes are real? All of them.

We separate without plans, without kiss, without words. I return to my seat in the truck parked near the entrance of South Gate where Portal Booth serves.

Babble exits Portal Booth waving a paper contract in his hand as he enters the truck.

Ha, they still use paper in the evolved world, I smirk.

Babble smiles like a man vanquishing arrest.

I never thought it would happen. Babble said it would, he talks a lot about everything. We wished it to expand our experience, and now we will. We are to be Observers in Simpatico. There will be no reporting to the rest of the world. No more Mohamed and Maria.

Three weeks off before returning for a six-week contract observing Simpatico.

Contract will be extended or not after that. No permission to tell anyone, not Society, not Simpatico Residents, only Portal can know.

Of course, we will tell our wives, not our children, thinking our wives can keep a secret, help us with this secret in case the worst happens.

Wives know everything and nothing. They know some of our darkest secrets, yet we hide some of our nearest enigmas.

I stop near Absentine.

She stalls towards me. She simulates a man masturbating, says 'Every day, think of me.'

She kisses each of my ears loudly 'Go now before I kiss your lips and run away.'

She turns aside with tears in her eyes.

I lift her forehead. Our noses brush softly. Her lips rise slowly.

We kiss deeply. Our lips smack as we break away. We both laugh glaring. Her fingertips trace my arms.

My shift is done. Surprised if I visited her for five minutes a day. In the future how many minutes a day will it be? You like what you cannot have. Why can't I draw her away to my hotel? Come now. A Simpatico Resident will not venture into town.

The culture does not call for it. Could she extend her day pass and visit on her day off?

She has agreed to be a Simpatico Resident not an Earthly Society subject. I hadn't even asked her to leave, only suggested meeting. Soon inside Simpatico, there will be no quick seductive holding. It will be seduction.

Project is done.

Babble and I will return for six weeks as Observers in Simpatico. Enough time to simulate in the population, enough time to fall in love, enough time to be harmed, enough time to be celebrated, and enough to time to face death. As fascinated as we are the opposite wariness flares.

Babble worked hard every day pocketing all the positive information he could, and the negative cancelled out. He was true, gave Society contractor what it needed. With Simpatico he never crossed the line he did not dictate a superior attitude. He did his job well, starting early, leaving late, and working through lunch breaks. Dependable. He's done all this with the goal of being paid in Simpatico and visiting Studio.

7

SOLAR FLARE, TIMING, distractions, distance, finance —
I don't have the answer. I want to see you, Absentine. Waiting
is always the answer. When I return, I don't want to wait any
longer; live now. A spirit haunting me, her eyes glisten, her smile
spurs claiming a mad man's sphere. If ever you think I copy
wrote this than another has also felt the same, making what I say
undeniable.

Damaged, stoned, they walk broken standing next to death.

The enviable.

I call my wife and break the news. She won't care. I'm coming
home then returning quickly to work. She is supportive. My
children understand.

I'm going home as empty as I've ever been.

I will walk through the door asking, "Where have I been". Seven
months is not a long time, but it is.

This is difficult for us thousands of kilometers away and still I feel
you Absentine. You are in my soul, crying in my eyes, terrible is
you thinking of where I cannot be found.

Desert woman, are you now at peace? tell are you still with me
when I travel?

Absentine, we can't be together I will become lazy in household chores, and you'll be nagging. We will be caught in a crossfire of spending decisions not ever fulfilling our personal needs. Codependent and dishonest. Jealous. Silly arguments. Disgusted, wondering if we'd made the accurate choice.

Or we could live separate and think of each other, point to our invisible minds. Or we could just fuck until we tire of each other and think it again for the rest of our lives.

Fuck once, maybe best for us. Twice!

She isn't even that pretty. She is remarkable.

All my failures vanish with my wife's words: 'You will soon have enough money... you can work for fun. You will not have to work at what you don't like. You'll be a millionaire twice.'

A double millionaire!

Spit on my breath

I hoped my wife would be distant fat uncaring cheating, so I could finish her.

She is beautiful. Smiling, considerate, in shape, we make love for hours. Good thing. Without her I'm not a double millionaire. Opposite of everything I thought, and why shouldn't it be.

The word "Millionaire" is devastating.

What will I struggle for now?

Give me the cash now, disappear does not resonant. I love my wife as much as before.

So, this is life. I will start new with her — win or lose we'll start this time with a heavy bank account.

A millionaire. Our investments doubled up since I've been away. Rich for our demographic our predicament.

Not fighting with my wife is worth a million. We haven't fought this first week.

I can't say "millionaire" if I finish her. I'd only have half, spend it fast with a tricky one, broke working as I do now.

Still, I'm chained. The money sits, value loading up, can't touch it yet.

How lovely is home, it is only passing time to return to the adventure of Observer.

Return to work is deliberate. My wife says I could stay home for a year. I don't listen, my mind already trained to leave.

My first week home lasted forever — spiritual, mind-blowing. The last week home quick cruel.

I return to Simpatico with a face of confidence.

Babble says he's been waiting years to hear me say I'm done working jobs I hate. 'I expected you to be a millionaire soon after I met you. What took you so long, did someone die?'

'No. It's all my own.'

He cries with laughter laying his hands on my back in joy. 'The topping to our ice cream sundae treats with passes to observe Simpatico.' Then he stops and thinks, 'Why did you come back?'

'Haven't cashed the million yet. Have some things I'd like to see through.'

'Absentine,' he breathes.

'Studio' I sigh.

Simpatico

———

INTO THE PLANET. PEOPLE knew before it happened.

Call it vibrations call it hidden messages, calculations in their minds. Come build, come Serve. It was no question, it was quest, it was spiritual, written in the future, read now.

In their minds, their belief, they are to be prophets. Wise.

Evil is welcome in Simpatico because it is one of the emotions, one of the questions, one of the answers in life. It is the extreme that is forbidden.

We are in for fortune or pain.

Babble smolders relieved, the wait is over we've already checked into our rooms at Visitor Complex.

Will this be comedy or enlightenment? Observing implications of the innovations.

We've been lodged at the hotel in town for three days of bellyache. New contract, new physical and cognitive check-ups, including sexual transmitted disease.

Our guide met us every morning. That's his name "Guide".

He is native to this area. A techno geek. Amusing insightful. A Simpatico Resident, yet his home is outside Simpatico territory. Married, has children. A most handsome honest balanced man.

We wait on the sidewalk entrance of Visitor Complex for Guide to greet us for our tour of Simpatico territory.

A woman nearly knocks me over with a tight hug. She sticks to me. I can't see her face I can feel her spirit.

Her voice is licentious, refreshing.

'Absentine.'

Full intense our bones mesh. Her breasts fuse to my torso. Midsections bump hold. After our embrace, hands to forearms, wrists to shoulders. We can go anywhere!

Fuck (me) you today.

'What are you doing here, I can't believe this.' True exuberant. Screaming giggling.

I can scarcely stand it, too refreshing, too positive. 'Observer — observing life in Simpatico.'

Guide arrives in a remote car for our tour.

I back away from Absentine. 'I must go observe now.'

'Find me' she chills.

I join Babble and Guide.

Remote car drives on the main grid that travels the circumference of Simpatico. Secondary roads are connected to the main grid. One main loop with paved arms to different districts. Numerous unpaved trails.

Is this life? I wonder.

The best of life.

Jubilant has landed.

Advanced commitment to mental and physical health. Residents are serviced like valuable equipment. Simpatico attempting designer health supplement technic. Designed for strengthening mind and physical wellbeing. Resident designed health supplement, combating and protection from oncoming disease. A Visitor and Guest may volunteer to have designed health supplements once they've passed probation and signed contracts—a brilliant incentive for Guest and Visitors to return.

Guide reminds us, 'Designer health supplements for nonresidents are a watered-down version. We can't provide you with something that may not be legal in your own country.'

We both agree with Guide's claim.

Guide exclaims, 'A Resident provides a service. If a Resident wants to clean, a Resident cleans. If they want to change the world, change it. Brilliant!'

Infrastructure archaic. Pretty things not a priority. Flowers, trees, are placed without measured concentration.

Random.

Buildings come in boxes, rectangle, square, hexagon. Cute design, built fast, economically. Uniqueness is found inside the buildings. Residents are not limited to one place of stay. If available accommodate another condo, cabin, or apartment. Condos come in configurations of one to eight person spaces, some with yards. Apartments come in one to four person spaces. Cabins, as many persons as can fit, plus livable outdoor space.

Residents travel directly from the airport in flying passenger taxi. Everyone else on a bus or van transporter. Resident, Specialist, Vacationer have airport use. Visitors through South Gate, Guests depending.

Only thing missing is space travel — waste of money. Simpatico too far behind.

'We have underground complexes too!' Guide gushes.

North Villa, the remote car stops.

Beyond North Villa we are not privileged to enter.

'What's beyond North Villa?' we both ask simultaneously.

'Beyond North Villa is Separation, called Atmosphere... where citizens can reside in Studio, called Studio Port.'

Babble and I gawk at the wall speechless. We both think, let us go observe Atmosphere.

Guide breaths. 'You cannot Observe in Atmosphere. Not yet. Ask Portal later, after six weeks service.'

'"Atmosphere" is a strange name for a place,' I comment.

'Atmosphere is where Bandit's stray.'

'A Bandit is a criminal?'

'No. A Bandit can be a good person, don't let the name fool you. "Bandit" is just a term that came to be for the illegal, the denied, the expelled. Atmosphere allows Bandits. Portal says it is a necessity, offers them jobs to Serve.'

We understand.

'Stop thinking about over there, think here.' Guide schools. 'This side we call Simpatico, the other side we call Separation or Atmosphere. It's all Simpatico. Six months ago, we all lived together, and then we separated.'

'Why?'

'Everything separates.'

'What is the difference between Atmosphere and here?'

'Residents in Atmosphere can control create their simulations; the user has input.'

'How many Residents over there in Separation?'

'Same as here, more or less.'

'How many is that?'

'Don't know. We are still accepting.'

'What's Studio like?'

We must experience, we are certain. Babble and I amused.

'Depends,' Guide swears. 'Studios have been updating.'

'Oh' we both gasp.

Simpatico questioning meaning of life with accessible goals distributed around the globe. You can't do whatever you like, but you can ask.

If skills hobbies can't be done in Simpatico, the Resident has the chance to import the want or travel to meet the need. Just ask Portal and provide a reason.

'You must understand a Resident isn't interested in the outside world. Everything they need is here. Residents are the angels protecting the Simpatico design.' Guide smiles... his testament repeated, 'Never underestimate Simpatico. We have something that can't be seen — an energy that is a different dimension.'

'What about Simpatico cell phone service, and internet?' we look towards Guide.

He smiles, 'You have no need for Simpatico cell phone service, except for trouble. Do you want trouble?' He laughs.

Yes — we want trouble.

Guide continues, 'If you need cell service ask Portal. Have a good reason.'

We have a good reason.

We let Guide resume schooling us, 'If you must contact someone in Simpatico or outside Simpatico you can use the communication service at Visitor Complex. Internet is available for non-residents if you have the app and service. You don't have service. You have service at Visitor Complex.'

'Good. I can use the communication app there.'

Guide glares at us, his eyes sparkling, 'Each citizen has a personal relationship with Portal. It could be a diary, a confession, a friend, a sister, brother, father, aunt, a complaining mechanism or ego builder. Their relationship is their relationship. And the best thing is Simpatico Portal answers back — affirms or disagrees. Some use it to gossip hourly,' he chuckles to himself.

'And you?' asks Babble.

Guide thinks then answers confidently. 'We as Residents must take the time to input our Server responsibilities. Simpatico Portal is my workmate. Portal helps me get through the day as my personal guide. I do not have a schedule with Portal. Sometimes personal some days work related. That's it.'

Babble and I don't think this Portal relationship is stupid. We both wonder if this relationship with Portal will happen to us.

Residents communicate to Portal on their own devices. Babble and I will need to communicate with Portal at Visitor Complex.

'Tell us about reporting to Portal?' Babble and I both request.

'You cannot just write words to Portal — sometimes the words are misinterpreted. You can speak — though Portal may interpret the message unclear. Sometimes you need to explain again what you told or asked. It is the best way for humans to interact. Sometimes you need to wait and explain what you meant again. Time to reflect is best for interpretation. Portal will repeat the information you input. If you and Portal agree the information is correct, then it is processed. Portal does not like mistakes, it is sometimes proofed by humans.'

Our guide has spoken.

Guide goes on, 'Security is a problem — expensive. Simpatico donates expensive equipment to the local police for testing and use. Local police don't complain when we call them. In fact, they rush to defend Simpatico.

Vacation and Guest Resort has in-house security armed with tasers. Tourists, Vacationers, and Guests feel safer with security. Simpatico has thought of everything. And what it hasn't thought it updates.

Residents are more acceptable to being fenced in than seeing weaponized remote mobile and drones from a distance. Mobile and drones are ready to deploy if needed. We're working on advanced non-traditional weaponized security.'

Can't get away from that.

'We are inventing seamless security. We will still need to man, the AI. Humans can't just have fun, experience, and learn.'

'And don't forget Observe,' I voice.

We chuckle.

'They, the world said we couldn't survive without weapons — but we will. A gun free society — except for sport. We use a nearby hunting lodge and shooting range for sport and hunting trips. We have some hunting and archery enthusiasts; we don't need an army — not yet.' He laughs. 'Besides countries of nations that have invested, protect us.'

Simpatico designing testing security and weapons that don't kill but subdue. I suppose you could call it mind control. Is it brain control, human cell control? Neuron control, I've heard.

Aliens may use mind control. Humans could use brain control. Advanced AI, human cell control I suppose.

Does that make sense? Does the mind flex to behavior faster and easier than the brain does? Is an illusion created for our mind from the outside, or is it created inside our brain for our mind to experience.

Fool with the mind or fool with the brain.

Does the brain create the mind?

No, no, no, there is no brain without the mind. The mind is external creates all. External central intelligence. Simpatico.

Do engineered human cells create everything?

What I want to know is: will security be had externally through the mind, or internally from the brain? The mind would not even know all is from the brain. The brain unaware it is shaped by the mind.

You could also say mind is internal and brain external, depending.

Is human intelligence inborn or received to soft tissue from the unknown — soft tissue absorbing superior intelligence.

We are the growing intelligence of the galaxy, each of us a solider to our construction of superior intelligence. Intelligent enough to have our chores done for us. Intelligent enough to create our own galaxy perhaps create another species. That species, in its growing infancy will look to us as Gods, not knowing what and who we are. Though underneath it all they'll know somehow, we are here, there, everywhere.

'We will expand to another galaxy, another pattern, and that species will promote growth, expand, create another galaxy, and on and on. Some dissolving some excelling,' moans Guide.

I'm kind of tuned into what Guide says.

Flowers.

Insects.

A million experiments.

Spark, explosion, vacuum — each drop in a lab becomes an infinite expansion of nothing that appears microscopic but inside the microscopic drop is a universe that can't get out of itself. Never finding the end because it circles, changes again. You don't even know you were just there.

'Do you have a Senior Complex for the Elderly?' I ask Guide.

'Sure, there are a few old folks here. In fact, Simpatico is experimenting Studio for experienced souls. Nobody retires in

Simpatico. Seniors are fully integrated with extra recuperation time off from duties.'

First day done.

We toured 26 kilometers today: South Gate, Groves, North Villa, East Link, and some areas in-between.

I'm so happy, I laugh.

2

———

THE HUMAN CELL IS THE ignition, the brain is the file cabinet, and the mind is the viewing instrument. My first thought of the day.

Five days in I'm stable; it happens that fast.

First day: adrenaline.

Second day: tired.

Third day: learning.

Fourth day: do as you like.

Fifth day: is where I'm at now. I have a schedule, a plan, a circuit I visit, in time this will change.

Why hasn't Absentine knocked my door? I'd be disappointed if she did; bang her and leave her, it would be over. She's following the script.

The other evening, I could see Absentine at distance. She stood on an incline. Hands clasped together, her thumbs under her chin kissing her index fingers, then plunged to the sky. She repeated the gesture, feeling the universe is hers.

Tonight, I will walk in the cool towards Absentine. Talk to her.

Our accommodation at Visitor Complex is of ordinary standard. Reception and recreation area. Breakfast and evening meal served, take-away lunch. Private individual rooms.

In house preprogrammed television. In house Simpatico internet with ample entertainment, information, needs and wants. Indifferent, with no viewpoint of the surrounding world's happenings.

If a Resident must know what's going on in the rest the world, they should leave.

Visitors and Guests stay at Visitor Complex on long term and short-term contracts, sometimes just overnight.

A Guest and a Visitor are not classified as the same thing. A Visitor is confined to certain areas they work. They are not offered Simpatico residency privileges. A Guest has some privileges, depending on need. Babble and I are Guests, very good. Canteens are free to visit, eat. Lounge, restaurants, coffee shops, stores we pay, same as a Resident.

Hungry. Sundown.

Babble joins, we ride to the canteen near the incline Absentine posed in Grove's area.

Our electric bikes are parked. We walk towards the canteen entrance. Oh, did I tell you they gave us electric motorbikes to ride as we observe?

The bikes are fun with little chance of medical attention from a high-speed collision as the bikes are designed with limited speed.

Free I assume, medical attention if needed. I will ask Guide.

I nod towards a woman who stays at Visitor Complex. Babble chats her up each morning, a lot of touching, snickering. The woman says she'll meet us inside the canteen in a few minutes.

We enter.

I stare mad at Babble in comedic charm. 'You've come to meet her, haven't you?' I assert.

Babble looks at me in seriousness holding back laughter, 'Yes.' He goes on, 'She is a Guest on a three-month stay. She has a little freedom.' He laughs, waiting for a response.

'Nice hips.' I comment in agreement of his selection.

'I know. I always wanted a woman like her. Enormous hips. Different from home,' he grins.

I see why he is attracted; she's sizzling.

'You will exhaust yourself without a condom,' I comment, smiling concerned, sincere.

'I do. It was one of the requests we made to each other.'

He lied to me. He isn't just meeting her he has been seeing her. Fast, these two are.

'How many days have you been seeing her?'

'The night before last, and this afternoon.'

'Not worried about a child?'

'Nope. She doesn't want children with me, and I'm done with them.'

'Not scared you will hook up outside Simpatico?'

'Nope, not a chance.'

'Snap out of it,' I laugh with serious implications. Babble is a married man with three teenaged children back home.

'You'll do the same,' he laughs back in harmony. 'This place takes your mind away, enjoy the ride and forget about it. Watch yourself.'

As we eat, a commotion at the entrance of the canteen occurs. Absentine is involved, claiming someone tried to poison her. 'He added toxin to my health drink container,' she yells at a scrawny young man entering the canteen.

'No... not me,' the scrawny young man scowls. 'I'd like to, but I didn't do it.'

Didn't do it means he knows who did, I consider.

Absentine is nearly in tears.

A blessing to see her like this. I can claim insanity for all I wrote, said, felt, and dreamed.

With canteen management standing next to her, Absentine holds the health drink container up in the air. She points to the man whom she accuses as the culprit. He smiles, surely wanting to attack her for the accusation.

Absentine complains 'Why?'

The place goes silent, everyone wondering how this could happen. Health drink containers are usually sealed. Maybe eighty people in the canteen look to the canteen management for an answer.

I don't rush to Absentine's defense, I observe. Babble cool, his female friend mummified.

Absentine vanishes the scene. No look towards me.

After a meal of white fish, green peas, sweet potato, and walnut topped frozen yogurt. I say goodbye to Babble, and his friend.

Outside on an incline in the distance Absentine is meditating to the stars with two others. They stretch, hold breathing postures in strength positions.

An attractive woman walks behind me as I view Absentine from afar. The woman speaks in a clever honorable voice, 'She is close to prayer. Good thing she does her lotus position to prove meditative. Harm you know for Societies popular religious prayers.'

I kind of motion in agreement, as if I understand what she's talking about.

She continues, 'I do it in my room. My own invented prayers — sorry, I mean meditative positions. No cause for questions or poison, less risk. But she wants to show off out in the open.'

I'm waiting to hear more. She falls silent, lost in thought.

I smile and turn briefly viewing her side profile. Attractive, fun in a black leather jacket, light beige slacks, glowing dark brown hair, medium height, a body that consumes. She laughs out loud on her way to the autonomous van bound for North Villa. Some kind of inspiration this one is. I don't know if she is crazy or sane. Sarcastic appeal is surely not sane. She places her hand in the air and waves goodbye like a celebrity. She instructs the self-driving van in hilarious tone, 'Driver take me to North Villa.'

Guess I'm to visit North Villa soon too.

Seriously who is this wondrous woman? Is she the poisoner? The case is now clear: Absentine poisoned in warning for her meditation which closely replicates popular Earthly prayers.

An oasis filled with escapes, dreams, and false wellbeing. Desert woman, will you live long enough for us to greet. Suddenly, I have an excuse to ignore Absentine. The answer is this waving, torturous, wordy dream woman in a black leather jacket. Am I wrong? I have not seen her face near to mine. Is she possibly another phantom as Absentine? A mirage. This time I don't think so. I created Absentine out of thin air. This young woman knows something about me.

Absentine slows near me sulking. 'I'll talk to you later.' Gone.

How'd toxin get in her health drink container?

Every afternoon Absentine picks up her pink health drink container on a refrigerated shelve, labeled with her name.

Wreaked in an instant my thoughts of romantic. Lust has not dissolved, desirable sex still splatters, I admit.

Why can't she wear nice clothing, be pleasant, behave, have others surround her adoringly?

Babble says Absentine is fine but not worth the bother. He's found easier meat.

Guide says medical expenses in Simpatico are taken care of by Simpatico (cheap). Billed to us, docked off our funds. If a serious injury or medical problem exists — transference to Society emergency, expensive. Fortunately for us, Simpatico covers medical insurance coverage during our stay.

Life in a greenhouse. Optimum growth.

A portion of a Resident Favor receipts are kept in digital wallet, readily changeable to currencies of the world if ever a person leaves. My Favors are exchanged, taxed, and deposited into my wallet. The exchange rate is outrageous. Simpatico blames Society. I still make money, though a little less than before, I'm okay with it. Simpatico is far more enjoyable with added confusion.

3

———

HOW MANY ARMS DOES the earth have?

The silliest thing I've heard is sending rocket ships to space to figure out existence. Too far gone. Answers are nearby. By the time we get the information it will be wrong and by the time we get the information back we'll be gone. Send a microscopic retrieval signal to the mind... try that. I know it will take almost as long.

The human cell, examine it.

Reverse engineer.

Where is the mind?

Everywhere.

Vacuum slingshot travels fast.

The brain small, the universe large. Same thing. Reverse them.

Concentrate on detection on the near unseen the unheard instead of way out there with your rocket ship. Aliens are right here mister. You can discover the past if you like — easiest for you to do. If you can trace out the past, you can predict the future, or so they say. I don't believe the past tells the future well.

The simple answer examines the microscopic sparks that occur inside us and then consider the same results in larger scale. The human cell is connected to the universe. Travel that lane.

All the answers inside our exploding mind. Just a thought as I look to meditate towards the stars like Absentine does.

Did you see when the two black holes combined?

Answers are in-between the scene. We may not understand what we think, but we have thought and try to create what we think. Many have already thought the future, the present, the past — it will take another calculation to build the thought, but not the random, the random unknown.

I venture to North Villa, a place of apartments, offices, the gateway to Advanced Experimentation.

I walk Main Street, a lounge, a restaurant, a store. No mystery woman. Is she in an apartment overlooking me? Maybe.

I return to South Gate. Sleep.

Up out showered early to Observe. I want my observation hours in quick.

I return to Visitor Complex for late breakfast.

'Come here you,' I hear voiced in front of Visitor Complex.

The mysterious assassin has spoken. Today, she isn't wearing a leather jacket. Instead, she has on a tank top and shoulder sweater.

She sits sipping what appears to be tea and chews on a biscuit.

I'm hungry too.

The assassin, 'Did you know there is an old woman at a store that serves the original, the best designer tea if you have the correct number of Favors and a pleasant smile. She'll even design the ingredients for you. Nobody else can do this.'

'Does it have a nice taste?' I humor her.

'No' she grins. I move closer to listen. 'You never get what you desire. That's why a person keeps drinking it. Sharper ideals of perception, fooling you. Clear vision beyond reality producing truth, fear, or something you never expected.'

'The old woman is clever.'

'Clever. Most don't believe even when drunk and saw truth. They think they disbelieved. A spell, a potion; they sometimes call her a Witch. We have no devil in Simpatico but in the future we could. The old woman understands this.'

'How do you know so much?'

'Because the old woman is my friend.'

'You come down here to South Gate to drink designer tea, then wait, sit, and trip?'

'I'm here on reconnaissance, and you are Observer.'

She is fantastic, tricky, full of questions she knows the answers yet wants to hear you say them. She is striking and isn't nice about it.

I snap out of it. 'What is reconnaissance?'

'Oh, you know getting a feel for what's happening here in Simpatico. Scotch Cola, is my name.' She extends her hand sweet and dangerous.

I clasp her hand. 'Lucky Ce, is my name.'

'Have a drink' she says lifting the cup to my lips. 'Don't worry, nobody is looking. I'll keep an eye out.'

'Is it illegal?'

'No... but you are a Guest. Maybe illegal back in your home country... you understand they don't offer this type of refreshment at home. It's a Simpatico thing.'

The designer tea tastes like burnt leaves. Instantly refreshing, the opposite of what the taste tells the brain to anticipate. She encourages me to take another drink.

'I don't live in Simpatico.' Scotch Cola states blank.

'You are a Bandit?' I presume in words.

'No, I'm not that type of Bandit. There are no Bandits on this side of Simpatico. Bandits stay in Separation near the creek. I have an apartment in East Link. It is where I Serve. Have you been to East Link?'

'Drove in, stopped at the Lunch Inn.'

East Link, the hip linking Separation where Residents visit family, friends, lovers. A shared Hospital. Vacation Resort. You can enter East Link from Atmosphere side or Simpatico side, returning the same way you came in.

Scotch Cola frowns, 'Simpatico looks terrible if you come from East Link.'

Yes, however the whole reason you become a Resident of Simpatico is to get away from places like East Link and Vacation Resort.

'You should come to East Link sometime,' she says, squeezing my hand.

She takes a sip from the cup, then holds the cup up to my lips, encouraging me to do the same. I hold the cup and take a sip. She releases my hand and shakes both her wrists at the same time, like a dance. Smiles laughing, 'Lucky Ce! They said you are funny, but I didn't know you seem kind of serious too. I can see it will take some work to lighten you up soften you down.'

I pass her back the cup.

'Scotch Cola you come on too strong, wicked, cool, good. If you were this cool, you'd be stupid. Stupid I think not.'

'Ha-ha, you are funny. They were right about you. Go ahead and ask me who?'

'Who says I'm funny?'

'Everybody. Everybody talks about you and your friend the other Observer. Even Portal says you guys are funny. Funny in a good way.' She pauses a moment, 'Simpatico answers to no one. Computers don't have feelings, friends, nor relatives. Bribes, crooks, hacks can't infiltrate Simpatico.'

'Why can't it be hacked by crooks?'

'Because Portal says so.'

We are reflective in silence.

'Have you heard of no-man's-land?' She asks after the moment of peace.

I indicate yes and no. Society called the border area no-man's-land before the fence was constructed.

'It is a barrier between realty as we know it, and nothingness as we know it,' she reveals.

'What is nothingness?'

'Nothing, nothingness. No one knows because they are afraid and return to reality. In-between reality and nothingness you have no-man's-land'

'The space between life and death?'

'Nobody knows. That's the thing.'

She leaves it as that. I have no more questions.

'I must go Observe now.'

'You are observing. You are observing me, yes?'

'Yes.'

'You can't get a better observation than me.'

'I guess.'

'Is this not an event?'

'Kind of.'

'Come. Come with me? You can write it in your report. Portal gives you direction, correct?'

'No... not usually. We check in every day, report.'

'Come to the park with me. Fill it in your report now.'

'I can input my report at Visitor Complex.'

'Go fast before full designer tea kicks in. Otherwise, you may not be able to input your report today. I will heat up the rest of the designer tea at the store up the road, then we drink together. Hurry, twenty minutes.'

I produce my planned day report in five minutes. I spend another ten minutes eating breakfast plus five minutes freshening up in my room.

Scotch Cola is waiting for me with a remote car.

The last of the designer tea is shared. We travel west towards Groves, where condos, cabins, schools, and a Health Centre are located. North of Groves is Advanced Experimentation section.

We step out of the car and walk east a half kilometer off the main road to a park.

The scene is dramatic: pools of water for relaxation, hyperbaric chambers, tree houses, mats on the ground.

Paths travel for many kilometers east, north, and a few kilometers south.

Scotch Cola takes my arm, we rest on a wooden table. We are to "visualize" she instructs. Our hands touch in pose. She closes her eyes, I close mine. 'Think of me, and I'll think of you,' she orders.

Thwarted by her touch, I don't know what time it happened. I was trying to concentrate on anything other than sex. Unannounced during this lapse of time Scotch Cola stood up walked fifteen meters to a hut.

She sits yoga style.

Am I supposed to be thinking of her? In visualization, you are supposed to think of breathing or future success, aren't you? I stare past her. I close my eyes. Gaze with my inside eye.

I open my eyes.

Scotch Cola's hut is covered in ice and frost.

The bottom of the hut begins melting fast, dripping to slush.

The hut burns in flames.

Scotch Cola appears as a devil encased in orange flame. She does not burn.

I close my eyes.

I open my eyes.

The flame subsides, the water vanished away. The hut remains.

Scotch Cola stands and walks over to me.

'Let's go somewhere else. Can you walk?'

'I think so.' No troubling walking, though struggle talking.

'You can't drink too much it will ruin your day, and you'll sleep. Move on, forget about what you saw. I will go back to East Link now. Nobody cares about your report, though you should put in your hours. At worst, you can Observe at Store of Information. Do you know where that is? It is where I heated up the designer tea. Just over from Visitor Complex across the street.'

I nod.

She insists we will meet again.

We walk to a remote car. She instructs the remote car to drive me back while she takes another car.

Out of the car I decide to ride my bike even though Store of Information is only a hundred meters away; I want to maintain the appearance that I'm out doing my observations. Once past this area, is Simpatico industrial all the way to East Link. Visiting workers are transported from town to Simpatico industrial daily. They put in hours for good benefits, and okay pay.

4

—

THE SIGN DOESN'T READ "Store of Information"; it reads "Star Natural". Illegible unless you are inches away. Advertisement-less in Simpatico.

Large bay darkened windows, quiet place. I enter. Silence is abundant. Peace shattered as the door closes behind me. Inside natural light is ample. Chairs, couch, tables, a Portal Booth. A woman emerges from a hall extending to a back room.

She looks affluent. Dirty blonde hair. Athletic. Shiny clothing. Out of my league. Then I think, I'm rich too. She's a different kind of rich... she does as she please.

I ask, 'Is this Store of Information?'

'Some call it "Store of Information" but this place is not Store of Information.'

'What is it?'

'This is "Star Natural" a place for Residents, Specialist, and Guests if they need guidance with input or output for Portal. I provide information. Kind of like Information Centre. You are Lucky Ce,' She smiles. 'I was about to leave.'

I wonder if every woman is beautiful in Simpatico. It isn't true, the opposite is true. I'm on the meet one beautiful woman and she will introduce you to another beat. The space is artistically pleasing.

'My friend said an old woman serves tea here?'

She laughs. 'The old lady is not here. Just me. What is going on with you? Someone gave you something.'

I hesitate.

She seems to know already, 'Let me see.' She moves close, turns my chin slightly with her hand to look at me straight. 'Oh, I know. Scotch Cola gave you her custom-made tea just out front on the road. No good for you.'

I can't speak. Her French-Canadian accent is comforting confident and absolute.

'Scotch Cola set us up. You want to relax for a while?'

'Yes,' I answer.

'Come sit.' She leans on a tall table with a stool next to it. I sit as offered. 'Now you forget about another girl is this true?'

I nod 'True.'

'Yes. I know. Well don't forget everything for her. I will offer you a soothing designer tea... calm you.' She leaves down the hall, returning in minutes. 'Have this drink, a modest design. Cola's brand is too wicked — enlightening sure, but you need to relax and have a nice afternoon and evening later. Her custom design is not for you. It is for her. Now I will cure you.'

The day is turning interesting beyond belief. I try to sip slow. I slurp quick.

'I've seen you around Vacation Complex. I know much.' She asserts.

I nod.

'Scotch Cola was just needing to get rid of you. It was all she could think of. Scotch Cola feels very good at first, but later, not so much.'

Her words her disposition is remarkable, she seems sane. She must be in her mid-thirties though her body has a younger shape. She does not seem thirsty; rather, she seems to be gathering thirst and satisfying it. A happy woman. She is completely different from Scotch Cola. Right off I can see we are on the same wavelength — we are disciplined, we will not argue. I will not fall in lust for her. I may dream of her, but I doubt it.

Some people you sense familiarity with. I think, perfect. Life is perfect. She must jog, do yoga, plus use a little weight machine. The worst part is she seems sensible. I'm not interested in her and her accent one bit. I'll listen to her, take her advice as counselor. All the time letting her think she is smarter than I am. Let her think she is a teacher in a league I've never been. This is my long game plan.

I feel younger today, an understanding of resolve. Create positive ingredients naturally and this is dangerous because at times the guilty parts of my brain create unhealthy ingredients. The problem with awareness is that you can solve; if you intend to solve all yourself you can also take the opposite direction and destroy everything.

A reflection induced with calm egocentric thoughts emphasized.

'Do you drink designer tea?' I ask her.

'No. I take my own costume made Health Supplement. It keeps me fine-tuned most of the day fading away by evening for a pleasant long sleep. Folks like to change their being and not listen to what Portal suggests. I listen.'

I smile softly.

She explains, 'There is a time for designer tea. Once you have experience you find the same results externally and internally without it... you understand. You don't want to be a fiend. A designer tea fiend. You have your weekend abuser and your afternoon causal user. You have your once-in-a-while user when it has meaning or necessity. If abused, it no longer works. Scotch Cola does not understand this.'

My next question is silent to myself: Does Absentine understand this drink?

After all that happened today, I'm thinking of Absentine!

'What is your name?' Is all I can mumble out.

'Call me "Chanel TV".'

'Chanel T—-V.' I stretch my voice. 'You have nice skin.'

She laughs. 'Losing my suntan. I swim every day at an outdoor pool on lunch break. Pool is next to Visitor Complex,' she twinkles. Talks about her store, how she opened it with two others. 'All you have to do is have an idea, a plan to execute, submit the idea, and voilà!'

'Very good.'

'I thought so. Lunchtime, no swim today.' She shades the room locks the front door, indicates we must move. I follow her to the back room. 'We have a shower room. Have a shower. Go ahead you'll feel great, refreshed. I'll brew you another cup of tea. Shower fast... clean. I showered before you came in.'

I shower and return to Chanel TV's company. She has changed her clothing to comfortable wear.

She positions a mat on a low sitting table for me to rest, presents a half cup of designer tea for me to test. Good.

Kneeling next to me now, her braless nipples team tender on my shoulder as she starts to massage my temples.

She relents rises, takes a glass of water. Asks kind questions of my life.

After finishing the half cup of designer tea, I lay back.

Chanel hums a song. Sings quietly. Soothing begins. Mending my body with her hands stroking my forehead, my arms. My legs are taken, stretched out — her hands haunt my outer inner thighs.

She goes to my chest leaning direct in front of my breath. She takes her shirt off.

Her hands roam along my shoulders to my arms pronouncing my hands up to her breasts. 'Good?' She breathes firm.

I quietly nod in little resistance.

She undoes my belt, and ruthlessly lowers my waistline.

'Better with your clothing off' emphasized by her.

I answer with my chin up.

She uses her strength to pull my pants off. Sleight of hand 'Steady,' she suggests.

Up my thighs, she is naked.

All my courage cannot stop her action. Tremendous. Her motion is superior to mine. Her hands hold my arms down.

Eyes glow, subtle adoring breasts.

Together.

I won't last—her devil action.

Her head shaking no, meaning yes, please, so unexpected is helping me best.

No scream. Clean heavenly.

'Inside me.' When she says this... I'm alive. 'Good,' she lies her head on my shoulder and sighs.

We are still.

'I won't be pregnant' she whispers. Encouraging. 'We can do it some more, later.'

In supreme faze mode. I stare blank unmoved at her request.

She rises to wash clean.

Dressed. 'We can walk outside in the park. Good for you,' she suggests.

'What about your store?'

'My partner will be here in ten minutes to reopen.'

'Long lunch break.'

'The beauty of Simpatico. I'll make the time back. Oh no,' she laughs. 'Three costumers were knocking at the door. We didn't hear a thing.'

In the woods behind her store, we walk in the park.

All her parts fine, no exaggeration a perfect 9. I could have done worse.

She's blunt direct, 'I needed to act on you, before someone else.' Our walking action stops. We look at each other motionless. 'You are not some heroic catch... you are a commodity.' She laughs offering her hand to my shoulder humoring me. 'We in Simpatico would rather have an affair with a Guest than a local. Less trouble.' Her suntan turns to blush, 'Sometimes women like to have a lover, believe it, or not. Besides, it will be winter soon.'

We hold hands for a few seconds as we walk towards a slim graveled road amongst trails of the woods. Our conversation balanced spare.

I have always liked measurements that are not equal because that is real. Perfect is nothing. As many times as you do something the result will be the same, getting there is the adventure. A hundred times, a hundred different ways. Empty and start again. You walk around for weeks and do not notice a thing, and then you see it.

A machine needs fuel.

Walk on water immortality.

It is unjust that I can feel a goddess, and there she is... how a fool I am. Cruel is the unseen world.

Have I lost my mind?

Have I scattered the world?

She could be wearing red, she is not.

She is wearing green and black. There is no denying I care, though I'm in shelter. Sheltered love, not full abundant caring.

It is a scene that I could never imagine. It is a seen as disturbing as I've ever been acquainted with. A scene with a woman I desire.

What I see will not stop this desire.

Absentine is the woman I see in the distance.

5

<hr>

A SIMPATICO WORK TRUCK is parked near a quaint closed-door hut. A skinny hostile man with light hair paces back and forth before bursting into the hut.

We are close to passing by the hut when a mustached man with a potbelly comes out of the hut smoking a cigar shaking his head in displeasure. The skinny man exits the hut behind him. The skinny man lifts his arms in the air in disgust. They look at each other in aggravation and begin to argue over a woman.

Chanel and I change direction as to avoid standing directly in front of the scene. We can hear and view them. They haven't noticed us hidden in the landscape.

I recognize both men, but I hope not.

'They have a woman in the hut.' Chanel whispers.

'Does this happen, often?' I sigh.

'Things happen, lots of no-good happens here same as everywhere accept different. You see how pissed the skinny man is?'

'What are they up to with the woman?' I inquire.

'Don't know? You are a good Observer. In Simpatico things get taken care of by themselves. Just leave them be — report what you must. You are Observer, don't intrude. Maybe a massage, maybe a debt owed, perhaps a designer tea reading. Unless we walk into that hut and intervene, and still, we won't know. Correct?'

'Correct. Maybe rape.'

'Don't stop them. They are Simpatico; you are from the outside world. What they do is between them. Keep your job. You are here to "Observe" not to save Simpatico people, remember.'

'I'm human.'

'Can't you see, they are not!' Chanel's tone is sharp, determined to see things the Simpatico way.

Is it unjust to observe and not intervene?

A woman walks out of the hut.

Absentine.

Chanel taps her hand to my chest.

Absentine stands between the two men, gesturing them to leave.

I'm not tense, nor lost in temper. I've established Absentine is in her domain.

The skinny man attempts to wrap his arms around her. She resists. He has been rejected. He may rape her later, though I doubt it. You don't rape a prize you'd thought you won. He looks hurt.

The potbelly man establishes, 'She doesn't want you.'

'Either of you,' she expresses vehemently.

He faints sad. The two men sulk for the moment... gather themselves in the truck. The truck starts up, rolls away.

Chanel and I stop hiding and continue walking on the trail.

Absentine walks back to the hut looking our way, recognizing us.

Chillingly silent, not only us, the entire desolate scene.

Why?

I look at Chanel, spy her eyes. 'I know her. How did you know?'

Chanel responds, 'Designer tea is truth seer. What you really want to know you find. Honestly, I didn't know. You can believe information flows freely and we intersected. Whatever you want to believe — that I'm evil or godly for being with you at this exact place in time. We don't know anything. Possibly she was teaching breathing meditation or inhaling mellow smoke.'

My mind drifts to places I don't want to go but be gifted to.

Chanel intakes breath. Breathes out 'Go talk to her. She is still in the hut.'

'Will you wait?'

'Come see me later.'

How much truth in one day? Is what I want to say.

'Go speak, go ahead.'

I'm enthralled in this compassion. Can't Chanel lie, so I can call her a lair and discover something no good about her. Perfect, every time.

Chanel informs 'I don't want you coming around as a regular to my place to drink tea.'

I break from her grip. 'You don't want me to stop by?'

She faces me keen. 'No, I don't need you bothering me like that. You can bother me other ways.'

I don't know which way. Romantic I suppose.

Chanel brushes my arm in sweet gesture, 'This is different I've told you to come.'

Her finger clears moistness off my brow. I try to resist, though I like the gesture.

She walks the path to her store alone.

I make my way. Without hesitation I enter the hut.

Absentine seated, knees up, clearing tears.

'Do you want to fuck me too?' she scolds.

'No.'

'Thanks a lot.'

'I mean — yes, not this way though.'

'So, you want to fuck me?'

'No. Yes. What am I to say? I'm not happy either.'

'Be my friend.' She looks positively to my eyes.

I'm silent.

'Give me a few minutes,' she sighs.

'Okay I will wait outside.'

She comes outside.

'You will ride with me?' She walks to an electric bike. 'Hop on. I will tell you everything... up the road we can stop and talk.'

I accept. Feel hunger for her.

'Hungry?' she asks. 'We can stop at a canteen halfway to my condo nice and quiet.'

'Drop me off — I can follow you on my bike.'

Absentine does not ask why my bike is at Star Natural.

She is an excellent human being.

We arrive at the canteen. We eat chili-con-carne and spinach. Drink water.

Absentine begins. 'The fat man kept coming around asking for me, and I thought why not, he tried to assault me once. Now I can have my compensation. Let him beg. The skinny man wanted to come along too, and I said no, I just want him, the fat man. The skinny man came along anyway, he'll be compensating me too.'

'Fair,' I say.

'When I saw you, I was shy, make it look like I'm a big girl.'

'So... he's not your boyfriend?'

She laughs finally. 'Nope.' She relaxes, talks more, 'When they tried to seduce me, I decided since they were asking for more, I will give the fat man the hut today, and then... take it away. So now you know I'm unfit, your wife needn't worry.'

'That is your idea?'

'No. It was never my idea. I'm blemished, doesn't matter now let them hear what they gossip. They will hear it loud now.'

'Why?'

'— I entice them. My plan is wrong I understand. Don't worry I'm not giving myself to them as they tried to take. You understand now, they tried to take. They have not succeeded, and they won't.'

'They have not raped you?' Instantly thinking, why have I asked this.

Absentine doesn't care, she answers the question. 'They try, they always try. I talk. I satisfy them to a degree with hope, with pleasure in their mind. With fantasy, with want, with chance. I play them until they will be destroyed inside and out by their own desire.'

'They will rape you.'

'They have already tried. They will not again. Their desire is too strong.'

Confusion is uninvited knowledge.

We go our separate ways after our meal.

I have observed more today than all the days I've been here, this side or the other side of the fence and none of it will be documented in my official report. I can document walking in the park and relax huts. The attempted rape? I can't say at this time.

6

CREATE A PLACE WHERE techno and scientific inventions can be tried. A place that is governed by people selected by computers. You nominate someone. The computer selects position for the nominee.

The Inventor of Simpatico met a Marketer, and she introduced the Inventor to a Technical Wizard. The Marketer then introduced a wealthy creative Businessman to them. The four of them jelled an idea of humanity together. A unique thinker, a brilliant marketer, a business titan, and a techno wizard.

The Inventor wrote the Simpatico paper then disappeared after corporate, private, public, and government support was secured. The Inventor said if it is truly an AI governed society the Inventor must disappear. He was never heard from again leaving the Marketer, Technical Wizard, and Businessman to realize the Simpatico design.

I slept like a cow last night, meaning I could have slept standing up. A very deep sleep, not counting sheep. I know the truth; cows lay down to sleep.

Babble tells, he saw Absentine close to the lake.

I suppose I can find her on top of the bluff later if I like. How long can my mind be on Absentine? I hope Chanel TV does not show off, console, befriend her.

I give Babble happiness with a story. 'I was held captive and raped last night. I couldn't stop it.'

'By a gang?' he laughs.

Funny!

'She kept saying "Yes you can" unbuckled my pants, slipped off her slacks.'

Babble demur, 'You weren't held captive or raped! Don't insult women. You were seduced,' he says from a frown to a pleasurable smirk.

'Yes seduced. I felt shy at the start.'

'Yeah... I got it, and during joy!' Smug.

'Extensively.' Both of us grinning.

Sleep.

Wake.

It's my day off.

Strolling the road, slim exercise.

Scotch Cola is standing outside Fine Café. For some reason I expected Simpatico to be farther technically advanced not naturally enhanced, the opposite of what I thought — almost alien. She must have known I'd be walking this path.

'Lucky Ce. You're supposed to take me for a drink,' Scotch Cola playful in tone.

'You are not going to take advantage of me, are you?' I reply, joking.

'No, I wouldn't do that to you. I'm here on reconnaissance, looking for customers for where I serve.'

'Really? Am I to be a customer?'

'Not anymore. You've already been recruited personally by me. They say I'm the best rep in all Simpatico. I'm in high demand... never consorting with the customers. So, don't come to East Link Relax Lounge, otherwise... well you know, I'll say good-bye.'

'Where can I find you?'

'In Studio, you like?'

'Maybe. I haven't permission to Observe Studio.'

'Think about it. Let me figure out the permission part.'

'I'll think about it. I don't want trouble.'

'No trouble. If you're uncomfortable, I won't take you to see Studio. Meet me here at Fine Café tomorrow, my night off, we will go to a lounge in North Villa for a drink.'

Scotch Cola seems to be an agent, either working against me or with me. Scotch Cola is a feeler, probing one's thoughts, smarter than a machine. Despite her allure, I'm more than tempted to have Babble meet her tomorrow night, if she agrees.

She agrees.

Forget strolling, I'm on the bike to catch up with Babble, update him on Scotch Cola's enigmatic behavior.

Babble looks amazed, 'You are already at that stage?' He drops his confounding thought display; a gentle smile escalates. 'You thought she was an assassin. Then you thought she was a computer. After that, you thought she was an agent, and now she is just a hostess for Relax Lounge.' Laughing ecstatic, 'A Simpatico Rep—she could be all those things and more. And now you think she will be our lover.' Intense laughter, tears shine.

'Babble, she is too much. Better than pretty. You may like to resist, but you can't. I don't want to fall for her. I don't even want to make love to her.'

'Interesting,' Babble intrigued.

'She isn't even beautiful, she is alluring. If she were just beautiful, why bother with us. An attractive smart powerful person wouldn't risk a woman like her.'

'Did you kiss?' he asks half joking, testing for his own motives.

'No, nothing. I don't want to follow her like an idiot for sex.'

'You give me?'

'If you can, you can have her. If not, don't be upset if I keep her.'

'Best man,' he taunts in humor.

I cut him off, 'Stupidest man wins.'

'Okay.'

'She can get us into Studio.'

'Really? What's Studio?' We both laugh.

'I don't know. But everyone wants to go.'

I ride my bike back to Visitor Complex, cruising slow in the areas Absentine may be serving.

Morning is interrupted by a gathering of monumental significance — a universal shuttering.

It's the greatest event in the history of Simpatico after creation and existence. The original Inventor the mastermind of Simpatico after hiding for seven years is making a public appearance. Only three people knew this person's identity.

Many believed the three wise ones: the Marketer, Businessman, and Techno Wizard invented this mythical person. While others said that is impossible, as these three wise ones haven't the abilities for the design. Then it was agreed Simpatico was a production of many people. The unknown original Inventor, an invention.

The Inventor is to speak today in recognition of Vacation Resort. It has been open for a month with official celebration and kick off happening today.

Chanel TV stands below side stage. Twenty-five Residents seated onstage, background for four governing reps standing upfront.

Applause, as the three original architects of "Simpatico" walk on stage, greeting the four governors.

The governors are up for evaluation soon. Evaluated — assessed every six months. Unless they've been reckless the governors last the first six months and then make appropriate adjustments. One governor out of the four casts a deciding vote among the other three.

After introductions, Marketer steps forward, dressed in a black skirt white blouse, her Afro combed down, she's aged since I'd seen her on media.

The Marketer approaches the microphone and says, 'This is him.' She introduces a man that has never been seen in public — the designer, the author, the messenger, the inventor of Simpatico.

An unassuming young man walks on stage. The applause is modest, as preferred by the quiet man. His idea expanded by three others in partnership and engineered by thousands, now he stands before us.

'I have come forward,' he says humbly. 'I thought people would worship the machine, then the machine became the government, and you have something to complain about. This is better than complaining of another human.'

When he says this, I know he's sealed his future and fate — not as a figure to be worshiped, but as a human who made it all happen. The others come across as businesslike, and he seems profoundly human.

From considering him insignificant, I now understand he is the inventor that made everything here possible. His thoughts and designs realized through others, making him the designer, programmer, developer, and inventor. His dream became reality with others capturing his vision, the enablers, Simpatico Servers.

Somebody shouts out 'String theory!'

Many people laugh.

The Inventor grins, clearly enjoying a good joke. The Inventor answers, 'There is no theory,' he responds. 'If you want a theory, you could say it's a thought process grown from person to person with curves.' He grins again. 'Just life.'

The Marketer howls, 'That's how I was able to sell it. Ever evolving. We can all grasp that.'

The Businessman states, 'We are here to unveil our Tourist section. Not just for the wealthy. School children and high school students will be funded for trips.'

Funded by the rich vacationers, I assume.

The Techno Wizard takes the microphone, faces the Inventor and says, 'Thank you, my friend.'

All four wise ones walk offstage.

The place erupts with energy in applause.

Slowly we all disperse.

I'm amazed, no, dismayed, no. I'm utterly underwhelmed while being overwhelmed.

What just happened? How has this happened?

As minimal information as I've ever seen at a political rally.

Like my job. Carry on, you are doing great, and if not, you'll receive the message personally.

Monopoly, even the simple man knows this is disaster. For the time being, brilliance.

Family members have attempted to rescue — or kidnap depending on your perspective their loved ones who have become Residents. Even if one is disillusioned is it right to force another out of their dwelling? Simpatico decides that, with the help of an appointed human.

What constitutes the best world, the best family design? This has been argued through the ages for all time. What does the world retain as good compared to Simpatico? Both provide you with borders. The entire world a guess and still the world lets Simpatico survive.

It is said that Simpatico is protected by the powers of the world for the sake of knowledge and experimentation.

Advanced human is true wealth.

7

―――

THE MOON IS SHARP. Spit on my breath. I want her.

There is no field, there is no polygraph test.

Breaking hearts bright fire our souls.

Big bang. It will never be.

Pollen lost in a gust of wind. No explosion, no random growth, not written in stone.

Go, go now, find new. Create, leave her behind.

What I once thought is nothing, sparks to air. What we had, did not exist.

Before Big Bang there was nothing, after Big Bang something.

Black hole.

I laugh to myself accepting the rules of Simpatico are maybe not so out of range. Absentine is vividly alive, almost disgustingly so. I see her as poor, just as I see myself — poor with richness in abundance.

If we don't become lovers, my heart won't be shattered. Meeting Absentine soothes a broken heart. The Earth has a new human, finding inner to a fault, diseased in vague. She is the new life, fucking the system by presenting new systems, pounding her own nails. She does it with mind sending signals. Somehow, I have captured her.

Leave me now before I fail.

Absentine's message: 'I gather my inside heart and portray it to the outside. I collect positive energy. I blow negative air to positive. Turn a smile, dismiss a frown. You are not a fool, the sane may try to kill you, laugh you, but in the end, you'll have your spirit high in the sky. Do you think you can be quiet and achieve the ultimate kingdom? Embrace the nonsense others think?' She adds 'We will meet,' though she doesn't specify when.

Babble senses my energy, my happiness, as we head to North Villa to meet Scotch Cola. He doesn't realize I'm still holding onto Absentine's message.

'You were ready for it. What a better introduction than Chanel TV. Any man would have done the same. She is stunning — an exceptional person. No hag with too much lipstick. No, you did it right.' Babble bubbling.

I remember the world back home doesn't matter, Babble and I are on another dimension. Alive.

The lounge North Villa.

Scotch Cola no longer engages with me, as she once did. Her attention focused on Babble, their eyes connecting. He is delighted to be drinking whiskey. Alcohol is rarely seen in Simpatico. Canteens don't serve, stores don't sell. Scotch Cola applies her grip to Babble, just like I'd thought. I want to throw something at him, knock out her hypnotism.

She hints if we want to Observe in Studio.

Babble and I look at each other deciding if we should ask her what Studio really is?

We are quiet. Let her spill, what Studio is.

She goes on about no-man's-land. We both lose track of her description.

Our question really is, how many Favors to get intimate with her. We are both thinking it, either of us wants to insult, or worse lose a chance to discover what Studio is.

Babble asks, 'In Vacation section can we penetrate Studio?' He had to use the word "Penetrate" what an idiot, bahahaha. Babble looks at me grinning; it will be funny later when Babble and I debrief.

'A Vacationer visits Studio and a theme is experienced in a safe time limited control. The length of stay can be for one or a few hours to a weekend if you have the funds. Only certain Studio themes are for Vacationers.'

Conversation, laughter, blah blah blah. I leave them alone.

Next morning.

Babble muffled ecstatic, he can't hold his excitement in. 'She's too much. She isn't pretty, but her eyes sway you. You may like to resist, but you can't. I'll fall for her, and I don't want to. Did you kiss, did she kiss you before?' He asks me.

'No nothing.' I answer stale.

'Don't give me more nothing. You are on a roll. Everything is nothing with you two. Like you said, I don't want to follow her like a fool.'

'You're already following her. This doesn't sound good; you already like her.'

Babble thinks out loud. 'She is captivating.'

'Why didn't you do something?' I ask.

'I don't know. She has a shield.'

'An impenetrable shield.' I laugh.

'Yah' he laughs — 'you felt the same way.'

'She makes you feel like you are hers, though you can't touch it. Now you understand.'

'She's a devil princess.'

'Princesses are a sham and that is why she is a princess.'

'I'm to be her Simpatico king.'

'Have you kissed her yet?' I tease. 'Just as I thought,' the end.

'I'm meeting her tomorrow afternoon my friend. On my day off.'

Wow, quick. Good Babble.

The beauty of Babble and me is Residents think we are more than we are. They see us as some kind-of knowledgeable beings, threats, saviors, or something else entirely, not understanding what we are. They wonder if we have more power than we do.

Simpatico, the genius. Much of what Simpatico does in advanced technology is sold to the world. Funded experiments. Secrets are kept unless the right price is offered and worth the revealed information. Simpatico knows that neither Babble nor I have any interest in its tales about how the future should unfold. That's part of the reason we were approved. We won't be dismantling its projects, only commenting on the general population that serves the machine.

I wonder why I'm even here. It makes no sense, other Guest, Specialist, or even Residents can observer and report. Perhaps I'm the experiment I'm being observed.

8

─────

I PURPOSELY DRIFT TODAY.

I have no reason why, maybe I have exhausted the previous areas I've observed.

A commotion near the shore of the lake. Thirteen people have gathered.

Yelling, finger pointing, near fists. Absentine is encircled.

Fuel is thrown on her. A man and a woman try to protect her.

Fear is something you want to run from with an eye looking back.

I can interrupt the scene and calm hostility. Observe and record is not in play today. I walk fast. A hero would run.

Before I can run, lit matches are thrown towards Absentine. She lashes out from the shielding man and woman protecting her. Absentine throws a hand gardening trowel at one of the match wielding women landing it against the woman's protecting arms.

Absentine's pant dress ignites in flames. She yells in long song as she dashes to the lake seconds away.

She plunges into the water. I think she's made it without burns to her skin, her hair seems okay.

The two women with matches throw stones as she treads away.

I'm on my bike, a hundred meters to a dock. I wave at Absentine to come near the dock.

None of the hostile gathering walks further or stone as she nears the pier.

I hold a stick with my hand, she grasps the stick; I pull her to shore. The crowd still huddled in conflict as she settles on my bike. We drive opposite the gathering of spectators.

I'm in a dangerous place.

As an Observer, I think I've only observed. Now I am offering help after the fact, this is natural, this can be accepted. I haven't caused an action or bombarded a scene. I have witnessed and with the results over I have offered assistance. Silly to even rationalize. If I'm to love Absentine like I claim in my mind, would my job as Observer matter? It would. Without the job, I have no Absentine.

We stop at her condo complex. She steps off the bike.

Her pant dress is half missing, underwear displayed.

'Why help me?' she asks.

'Because I know you.'

'Yes, I know you know me... why save me?'

'I can't stop what I feel.'

'You are stupid. Just because you feel something doesn't mean act.'

I shake my head slowly not understanding this stranger. I speak softly, 'Are you okay, are you burnt, hurt?'

'A little.' She shows me red marks on her leg. 'I'll be okay, just a little shaken,' she almost laughs. 'Happy to survive.'

'I think you could have harmed those two ladies more than they tried to burn you.'

'They deserved more.'

'What they did was awful.'

'It was. They hate me.' Soon she says, 'Thank you. You are kind, amazing, you are the only one in this god forbidden land. You know I asked to serve in your area, so you would protect me. I asked to serve with you... Lucky Ce the Observer.'

'Thank you.'

'Maybe you think I'm crazy, a no good. I'm not, I'm none of those things.'

'I know. I understand.'

She laughs, screams out loud in happiness.

'Yes,' she rejoices. Softly in my ear, she speaks, 'What I am inside is different from what can be seen.'

'I think the same,' I can't say more words. Stimulated beyond believe with her face brushing against mine in a still forever hold.

We break 'Can you get my things from work? My co-worker can handle things today, he is a good guy. I'll contact him. I don't want trouble.'

I return in thirty minutes with her things.

She is waiting outside, dry clothing on. She passes me food wrapped in a fine takeaway bowl.

'Homemade. You protected me today. A true hero.'

'I don't know. I don't know what I did.'

Near giggles, 'It doesn't work like that with everyone. Only you.' She gleams.

'Maybe.' I sigh, locked in pulse.

She rescues, 'I'm sure there are others that feel the same as me. A hero.'

'I don't know?' I concede, 'I don't think of others as I think you.'

She blushes. She has almost the answer she hoped. 'Write me a poem every day. You say you think of me. Prove it.'

In the evening a Simpatico Resident explains that the women who orchestrated the attack on Absentine was the wife and sister-in-law of the potbelly man who was attempting to seduce her.

Or as Absentine insinuates, they tried to rape her, and she fucked them.

Sometimes one day can mark all other days away, this could be one of those days I remember well in the future. I know I'm not smart enough to figure out any of what is happening in technology, mechanics, or medicine, inside myself I do understand. Simpatico Residents have an original aura, some are smart, others dumb; mixed prodigies of nothing. What sort of human Simpatico gathers is the displeased, the unfit, the seer of truth that the world is not how it should be. Specialists are neither Visitor nor Resident, they are the person most needed, some have been here from the start and have become Residents, while many have just stayed on as Specialist residing in East Link or North Villa stored as gold I'm told. The general Resident serves Simpatico — so the brilliant can get on with it.

A man the other day seemed interesting, smart. I thought I can learn something from him, and today I listen to him... and I think he's nonsensical.

We haven't heard people arguing or contemplating on whom, what, the divine is or has been. Residents resist past beliefs and think fresh, they all have one common thread: to answer the instructions of AI, worship nothing, only utopian laws. And what is utopian law? Whatever the hell you think is best. Is it better than the rest of Earth? Different. Something within they seek, they sought, and now they vision what they have always wished. Hopefully through technology this utopian journey can be realized. The natural laws of utopia are what the computer is designing. You become it, you live as it, or you leave. Debt is not an option for a Simpatico Resident, be banished. No show-off purchases, no unnecessary items.

Simpatico thinks everything. Religion and culture are factored into the analysis and not forgotten. If something is useful, it is used in the correct context, not for honor, tradition, or superstition — only for its usefulness. In countries of the world nobody can get anything done, following the rules of the system. In Simpatico proof positive is the rule.

I'm finding Simpatico simulation is living your inner life outwardly. Creating life has two approaches: built from the outside or built from the inside. If we build the outer world from our mind, brain, gut, is that real? All feelings created from what we've experienced. Or do we build from outside ourselves, and learn from it?

Do we want life created by us, or built for us to explore? Coming from within or absorbing learning from the outside.

Inside my mind fantastic — hollowness to think life can be this bright, beautiful, majestic, passionate, spiritual, animalistic. My ultimate human sensitivity; is torture always the best method to love? All the extremities touched. All the self-loathed. Dare the cell open. Something so new, so expansive, life is liberated you are toppled to another living level. Life has entered pain has reached elation has mind swirling blissful spell, has enduring unreasonable tales. I love, I hate, you swear, you yell hurrah out loud.

You are happy

You are despondent

You are in love. Lust?

Natural to her faith, be whatever she's to create... now I can understand the power it possesses. I'm learning how others are seduced by a faith.

Now, I will tell you something that in forty-six years I never thought would happen. I'm turning to you, crying not with tears but with happiness. I have turned to a new truth, a new spell, your actions your daily manners my body obeying you. Happy, happier than I never ever could have considered knowing it is not a miracle, I've been waiting so long for this.

Yes, to everything is how I started thinking today. My hands rose together in the air and then to my forehead, and then to my lips — I kissed your breath.

You already know I'm past human love with you. It hasn't an English name for what I feel, the human hasn't discovered everything yet.

I can write about you without sleep without food without surrender without glasses, erect and constant, you walk so straight I can find you kilometers away.

How can I stop writing?

I stop when I'm fulfilled — and then I start again.

To a man, I make no sense.

To my vision, it makes perfect sense.

Absentine messages me back: 'You are amazing you are a gift. I want something you have inside. Smile all day with you travel all night with you. Constantly happy.'

9

A ROCKET SCIENTIST, a clairvoyant, a devil — she haunts me. A man on a beam.

I'm leery with her most. If her passion is unleashed, biting, thirsting, tasting — I might not stop if it turns good. That could be an affair. All the indiscretions I hunger.

Even Chanel TV cannot stop her igniting my thunder.

Displaced.... Where is my mind? Overloaded, absorbing too much, needing to replenish.

Babble is missing.

Maybe Scotch Cola killed him. Fucked him to death. Is that possible?

I go to Chanel, official business.

Star Natural.

She moves away from a costumer she is serving. 'It's okay, you can be here.' Her frame sideways bright, 'I asked about you at Visitor Complex. I know you have been avoiding.' Her hand placed on my shoulder, 'It's ok.'

I don't claim innocence, this is not a woman I can fool with.

'I can't find my friend Babble. He was to meet with Scotch Cola for dinner the other night.'

She consults. 'No laws, no judge or jury in Simpatico. Absolutely nothing to base your punishment, risk on. Some people disappear from Simpatico. Sent back to their home country. Sometimes they are not. Have you been to East Link?'

'Briefly.'

'The designer tea you drank with me. Do you think that is free or expensive?'

I lift my eyebrow. 'I don't know.'

'You can't put a price on it. It is neither low-cost nor expensive. If you are making huge profit, business is shut. At rock bottom, people become zombie's, prisoner to their design. No rich, no poverty in Simpatico, only advanced human experience. Simpatico still has mean. Crime is in a family gene, passed down. I know your gene — it is royal elite traveling down low "Gypsy Sophistication" and now your gene is "Strange Fun".'

'What is your gene?' I look to her after listening intently.

'My gene is "Scorching the Rules... Justly". "Hot Fire, Cooling Sea" I'm joking. You think you are here for only a short time Lucky Ce; you are not. It starts that way. Here money doesn't matter unless you want to visit the rest of the world. We play sports, we have music, we have motorized machinery. Everything is here. You are the celebrity here. Are you a celebrity back in your own society?'

I ponder outer dimension... am I actually here? I could be anywhere listening to her. Transportation, please. Teleportation.

Chanel walks the floor, circles 'Many think the greatest artist in the world will come from here. This place was made for art. Everyone has a productive place to work, and acceptable technology. We haven't population. We will double in size and then stop at a final number within a thousand depending on the day plus the Visitors. The computer decides how many Visitors there shall be.'

'What else you got for me?' I intercept.

'Have you heard of the four? Up down left right. There is nothing else. Four ways to everything, four of everything.'

'Like an atom, it moves up down left or right.'

She smiles, 'You think your report isn't important, though it is. The information your report gathers and charts — you need to report the attempted sexual assault, plus consequences. You must wait for the whole story. Can't write "sexual assault" you must wait for the results, the aftermath. Cause and aftermath, the computer needs to learn otherwise man will be stopped from seeing woman, the huts hauled out because of one or two cases that would have happened anyway. Is the separation of man and woman needed? Let the case play out. Nobody wants to see this happen once. If seen once, you need the results. An Observer not a judge, until later — how cruel it sounds. Life is cruel.'

I indicate I'm fine. 'I was thinking about a tour of jail to see if Babble is there.'

'No jail in Simpatico, that's myth. If a horrific crime committed authorities meet the offender at the gates, that is last choice.

Simpatico takes care of issues itself mainly, once you've signed to be here your rights of the previous world are gone. Local authorities have no authority here.'

'What about Visitor and Guest?'

'Except Visitor, Guest, Specialist. You'll be met at the gates with local authorities, police.'

Real or not Simpatico knows if you are good or bad. You can be lazy with good results, that's okay. You can be busy and good, but if the results poor, trouble. Perhaps disappear or perform extra duties. If you want to disappear, think simple, think lazy, commit a crime, and you are free, not true. Somehow Simpatico knows and won't send you where you want to go. Residents try to promote no rich no poor. This promotion is myth, Simpatico has the "have and have not" this still exists.

'With no jail to visit, what will you observe today?' She asks as she plays her computer.

'Whatever I like. Observe the school system. Mostly though, I want to find Babble.'

'No. No school tour today. Today you will go East Link. Go find death.'

'I don't want to find death.'

'I would never do that to you. Go find your friend he is in the system, in Studio.'

'How did he get in?'

'Guest tester, with Scotch Cola. He must have paid funds. It is her job to fulfill contracts to Guests and Tourists, to entice funds from Society, and otherwise. He is not in a Vacation Resort Studio, he's in a Simpatico Studio... East Link Bay.'

'Is that legal?'

'Legal? You forgot already... no illegal, no legal. We have no laws, only response. We have rules as a warning... rules that can be broken and others that cannot.'

'Is Scotch Cola putting Babble in harm?'

'He put himself in harm. Two people together create one mistake.'

Two become one. One becomes two.

I leave to find Babble.

As I head towards East Link, a truck horn honks at me. It's Absentine, parked in her work truck just east of Visitor Complex.

I pull over.

Bad timing or great timing. My mind is almost a gaping hole.

She holds her hand near her head, and says, 'Stay out of mind Lucky Ce.' She's laughing, 'I wait your sayings every day.'

I should be weary of my thoughts of her.

Absentine tells onlookers I'm good, authentic.

She walks me somewhat away to privacy.

Takes her hand from her head and directs it at me. Pointing out that the sky is our meeting place. Our minds connect invisibly. She doesn't have to speak I can read... she can't believe our transcending transcendental meetings together or apart. Telepathy must have some kind of meaning. Two people thinking amazing lust at the exact same time. It is almost as if we are two strangers who have just met, engaged, and promise to greet in distress again.

Absentine looks closely at me, comes near. 'What do you feel?'

'I don't know. You are polite to me.'

'That's it. That's all you feel?' She sighs.

I won't say the expression "I love you" no I won't say that.

I only say, 'There is more.' I leave it at that. 'I'm late right now, I have to go.'

She turns away.

I know I have failed.

Struck her sad this day.

10

A TIDY SPARSE ROOM, everything needed to live. Lights dimmed. An astronaut chair inside a capsule takes main space of the room.

Babble curled up on a floor mat outside the capsule. He's missing the pillow. The pillow sits to the side of him.

I'd entered the Studio with a password from Scotch Cola obtained by Chanel.

Babble 'Wake up.'

'I'm dying.' He mumbles.

'You're not dying.'

He blacks back out.

I've killed my first man.

His eyes are closed. Good, not dead yet. Shall I slap him? Kick him would be good. I want to ask Babble what it is like to die. I don't have to ask.

'Don't be afraid... you are released from struggle, pain,' he sighs.

He arouses, rustles around, moans, accepts my help to the shower, placing his hands on the bathroom counter. I turn on the sink tap, cold water. Success. He fills his hands with water, splatters his face, neck, head, and hair. Straightens his back.

'You ready to leave here?'

'World? This world? No, not yet.'

'This Studio, Babble.' He politely pushes me out turns on the shower.

In thirty minutes, we are clear of East Link riding our bikes to Visitor Complex.

We converse in the parking lot.

Babble first, 'I'm addicted to death. Dying over, and over again. I was living to die in that capsule. Being born I remember nothing. Dying I remember everything. I felt fright and exhilaration, I embraced it. I will never go back, never.'

'Never go back where?'

'To my previous life, my country, my community, my home. All this work I do to pay for a house, that.'

'For your children, Babble.'

'Don't try it, Lucky. You will become violent, extreme. You already hate your life. Dying will put you over the brink. Your body will begin to crave the unpleasant as much as the pleasant. Maybe you will only crave pleasant. That is a big maybe because life is many feelings, equal in a day.

'Babble, how was heaven, there is no death correct?'

'Death' he says.

'And you, what are you Babble?'

'Me — there is no me. I'm many things. Like a cell, like the galaxy. Small and big together. Dense and spaciousness though not invisible at all, just in this atmosphere we can't be seen.'

'And the computer... are we the computer?'

'Computer is nothing. Tool is all the computer is... spaceship, techno, all made with human parts. I say human, otherwise you wouldn't understand.'

'Was I right we are living backwards we will invent ourselves with the technology?'

'Yes correct.'

I push further, 'We will create ourselves and find nothing at all.'

'Never ending. Life may end, but your particles of this universe are very enduring, very long. I could not travel to the end.'

'What about religion?'

'The stories, the Prophets are true to an extent for wisdom. There is truth in many things, absolutely we know nothing. Answers are ever-changing. The books teach you ways to deal with life, yes there are equations, laws to life... but also random. One book cannot tell all for every human.' He pauses. 'I'm going to die. I need to be simulated. My simulation will live on until the power is pulled.'

'You'd be dead Babble.'

'No problem. Alive, one with technology. Simpatico.'

I realize that it is Babble's interpretation. I consider the power will never be pulled, as his simulation will become part of the ever-present energy of the universe.

'In simulation you create, and others compete. I can't understand it, I have never been.' He stops explaining, seeing he's lost my interest.

He knows nothing.

Babble has been enamored with Scotch Cola. They've had sex, he's experienced death. This should be enough — fulfilled, ready to carry on in life. But no, Babble wants more. He spent all the funds he's made plus another week's worth. He's here for nothing.

We go to our rooms.

Later, sober in reality; he submits his report to Portal. He knows his brain instinct has been misplaced. Admitting he was so scared of death he wanted to die to forget. He would have killed himself if he could have during the horror of his first sitting of astronaut chair. Good thing he was locked in the capsule. At the end of day, he exclaims, 'Fuck! I won't go back there.'

'Where?' Casual I glimmer.

'Astronaut chair, inside capsule.'

He sounds like an alcoholic vowing never to drink again or a drug addict swearing off their fix. Babble believes that humans have techno parts inside us and future technology will have human parts inside it. Magical, unearthly. Advanced human.

'Depending, all becomes, never can I explain it.' Babble, exasperated.

'Try'

'A scientist — someone educated in this — can understand, and yet they can't. We become convinced of something that we don't understand.'

'Can't change the instinct of the primitive.'

Babble!!! Congratulations what a day.

A design develops into another design, ends the same, starts again.

When we are ready to learn, we learn, information provided installed in our mind. Advance when ready. A design is never equal until you find the equation ends the same.

Chanel TV, my nine. My next great habit.

Star Natural, I'll visit this afternoon. Get an explanation of astronaut's chair inside a capsule from her.

Chanel TV is clean — must be fantastic to eat. Staggering because I never thought we would connect, never thought my mood would curve to her the way it is curving now. I dissolve the thought.

I study Chanel. A normal person without needs.

'All tricks. Replicating emotions.' She explains death theme, 'Your mind does the rest. Vision is lost. By the time you've regained your vision you've traveled to another galaxy and back. Think you've died and come back.'

'Maybe.'

'I won't give you that trip Ce. The only way they can replicate death experience is to use a dying person... a person who has died. Mimic the path.'

'Thank you.'

'You will experience death over, and over again. Addicted to the flash of what was and is life. Addicted to leaving your human body in rising micro glowing particles. Your body is not dead. Your body nothing. Checking into another form.' She stops explaining momentarily. 'I haven't died yet. I can't tell you everything.'

I hesitate 'Why do we have to rise?'

'Because that's the way it is. When you leave your body, you rise, float, sparkle, thousands, perhaps millions, billions of particles.'

'I've done this before,' I claim. 'I've done this in the past without an astronaut chair or death simulation. I did it myself, or it happened to me, I don't know which, but it happened exactly as you say.'

Simpatico replicating what I and others have already felt.

Chanel explains, 'When we develop the technology people will be willing to die to experience it and then be brought back to life to try it again; a trillion-dollar business. This business will be forbidden, dissected, humiliated, and exercised to continue our mission that we haven't figured out yet. There will be an incredibly smart person to do both — die the death and live. Live and die because what if after the unknown there is nothing?'

'How do they do this technology?'

'Trust me, they don't know what the hell they are doing, just like life. Experiment.'

'Tell me what you think.'

'What I think is easy.'

'Tell me.'

'No machine, all in your head. There is no technology that can do what the human can visualize.'

Like-minded.

Residents revolve around a Simpatico computer, like a temple. As the angels of heaven, if they play their cards right, they can be that angel for all time.

Babble and I suppose if our contracts are to be renewed will depend on our willingness to Serve, to meditate in faith to Simpatico Portal.

You want wealth? You own what you thought, you don't own property. The beautiful places are everybody's and the worst spots are no ones. Socialism? Nah. The rich and powerful don't have to Serve Simpatico, they fly in fly out as Specialists, Guests, Tourists. Even the wealthy Resident can travel back and forth freely, if they fulfill a service. They all Serve Simpatico. Like that. Many Simpatico people return to their home country until they see what's the point; life here is built. East Link has a place for family, friends, lovers to visit — a junction of Resident, Specialist, Guest, and Vacationer. Scotch Cola's domain.

Chanel informs me Portal dictates Studio time to each Resident. She believes the techno is only our thoughts — no techno can make what we can't think — we think it, technology mimics.

'An atom has four movements: up, down, left, right. Where am I?' I look at her.

'Here with me.'

'Where are you?'

'I have made a hundred different moves — left, up, right, down, different patterns. I like where I am now. But after being with you maybe I'll move. Ha, ha, ha,' she laughs.

I study her.

'You don't think I'm pretty?' she asks.

'You are pretty, I never thought so when I first saw you.'

'You didn't think I was pretty?'

'I wasn't thinking about looks I was thinking of your actions and voice. You were pretty, already. I didn't have to think about that.'

'And now?'

'F—u—ck. Pretty. A pretty woman doesn't want to be told they are pretty because they know that already. And you do the opposite... ask if you are pretty.' I gleam.

'My turn Ce. You let your mind run away when what you need is right in front of you. You have grand designs that you chase instead.'

I smirk with a slow indication of "No... you're wrong".

'Quit chasing what you can't have, and if you want it get it. Be realistic.'

Frown. This lecture is all about Absentine.

Chanel knows about the torching flames on Absentine before riding wet on my bike.

11

COMMUNICATION, INFORMATION, gossip, talk — however you want to call it. A Resident friend has Simpatico news.

The wife and the sister-in-law of the potbelly man have been warned: if they bother Absentine, they will find repercussion. Maybe I was wrong to think unfavorable of Absentine. I'm still in her box.

The potbelly man desired Absentine, hounded her, offered her gifts, promised her advance. . . his wife horrified. His wife said, 'Of all the women, her? You have embarrassed me, why couldn't you have just fucked her?' she was heard.

He had tried to seduce her. He enjoyed the trying, too much. Absentine played him strong. He lusted her as a pleading man, a weak man, a fool — laughed at. Even his children wonder why.

The skinny man is already single. He escaped ridicule but it is said he too chased Absentine, catering to her with promises. Sent her funds and farfetched ideas to date as boyfriend and girlfriend. She laughed. The skinny man vanished from Simpatico — by Heavies, Portal, himself, or the unknown, nobody knows. Some say he is in Separation. Simpatico does not always send a Resident back to Society for misbehavior, it is depending. The potbelly man is not so lucky, he will have to face his skeletons in Simpatico.

The fat man loved her; the skinny man loved her. She left them in a path where the fat man's wife is disgraced and the skinny man vanquished.

Has she told a lie? Nope.

Did she steal? Nope.

Did she cheat? Nope.

Has she done something undeserving?

They attempted to rape her. She said 'Okay, stop. I will take you both, under my terms.'

They attempted to love her. Love hurts.

I know half-truths making no sense. I've made my decision. Not caring, I want more than sex with her. Even in Simpatico sexually assault is difficult to manage. Sexual desire is one that cannot be rejected easily. Anything can happen in Simpatico — there is no illegal or legal; morals are either upheld or rejected. It may involve Favors, namesake, residency, or the unknown for indiscretions.

If you look deep into human nature, anyone can become guilty. The mind begins to see everything as a possibility. Human can't understand human. Absentine can capture hold a secret; this is maybe why I like her. The mystery of Absentine — she has me. I've forgotten embarrassment, fled buried burned. I've forgotten about the attempted poison —just another day in the life of Absentine.

What is truth... is she awful? Awful is Simpatico, if anything goes it goes here.

When I'm alone I clasp my hands, breathe, raise my arms high, then return my clasped hands to my mouth and kiss my fingers raising them to the sky again. I feel wonderful. All the bad out, the good in. This has become a habit, following her.

She sends me signals nightly when I'm in my room. Absentine transverses my life, teleportation, her particles travel in waves above, around, and near. Absentine... I have hardly touched, yet she has shot my mind, inherited my system, downloaded my techno machine created to collide, to mix, she is not nice she is not good. I can enter a higher level of thought in-sync with the invisible the unholy I can't say magical because it isn't a trick. Absentine can fly in the sky, land in my room, attach, inhabit, entangle, maybe devil, maybe angel. I'm going to love her. I have loved her in the spiritual, the invisible, possibly in the techno machine.

Desire can destroy family, rid comfort, sweat money, hail chilling, dissolve self for lust. To find there is more to Earth. Visit the expanding universe, dream the experience for years, think of it on the day of death.

When dying "I have no mistakes" I want to say this. If I do not accept desire, pursue it, I will not know if I have made mistakes. Like the constrained, they do not eat what they want, and when they can eat what they want, they accept junk food.

If I do not pursue what I crave I will be left with women I can have easily in guilty passion of nothing... a desire one must fight, the unhealthy desire.

Do I want to fuck a true desire, or do I want to fuck many false desires? Many will try both, one, and many. Never attaining and the unattained is the same. Seek all desires, seek no desires, ruined, flawed.

Block me out dangerous woman you are everything I've never sought, how impractical, how lonely because it will never....

Everything has become clear I'm a spirit, Absentine a deity.

If she has a man I don't care because with her, I can have any woman. I can have all the silver, even gold. Absentine is my power station I can be anything. My worship came naturally. I've become a high bread of vision. She is perfect, she is all surrounding.

12

———

I PONDER: HOW CAN YOU experience death unless you are in the mind of someone that has died? Oh.... Is there anything else left in life? The mind is real visioning, and the machine fake — a fake machine produced by humans. We own the machine through our mind, built by our brains.

Seriously, does the mind know death?

AI decides who gets what. Simpatico is not equal. Equal has never excited. Humans have never secured equality; it is not in our nature. We can be content with chance.

In most societies, you work to use the material society supplies. In Simpatico you work to experiment life, all the depths of mind.

Simpatico people can live forever as a perpetual being. Yet they want to experience death too, to understand the cycle of life.... Every Resident understands this.

I bump into Absentine at the Fine Café. I'm on my work break. She is with a gathering of friends.

Absentine nudges, wraps her legs around my thigh's, pulls me in close. Public affectation. I smile lightly, unnerving to be tested, teased. Everyone's eyes astound.

Entranced. I find myself inside her lap. We embrace, declaring to the world we are one.

An indistinguishable man looks at us and says... 'What's this about?'

I call him indistinguishable because I haven't time to consider him anything other than average.

Life is full of contradictions. An environmentalist might have a small dog breed for no reason other than personal enjoyment. A fossil fuel lover might refuse to eat fast food. There is no perfect. Outstanding... I yell her name ten times inside my mind.

Delaying my break time. Absentine waves goodbye.

The indistinguishable man looks back at me in a confused angry state... why her and I?

We are going to have sex! My smirk flashed to his mind.

I continue with my day.

Guide is to come around and fill Babble and I up with dinner tonight — a Simpatico treat, a last hurrah together at the North Villa Lounge, as Guide is moving on. He will no longer be our guide. When we had a question Guide would say 'Go find out,' Babble and I like to mimic boisterous 'Go find out'. We like Guide.

I park my bike proceed to walk the fifty or so steps to the lounge.

A man shoulders me hard, knocking me purposely towards a light stand. My hands raised protecting from bumping my head.

I turn to see a non-smiling man that shouldered me. He is shorter than the larger mustached man standing behind him.

They look remarkable candid. It is the indistinguishable man that disapprovingly scolded me and Absentine earlier in the Fine Café. The mustached man standing behind him is the potbelly man accused of sexually abuse with Absentine. Can't miss his stupid mustache.

The indistinguishable man expecting me to answer to the knock I suppose.

'Watch yourself.' Is all I propose.

Fists? Uh. Not today.

We are both at extremes, our eyes threatening. What the hell does he want, sending prominent profanities I can't understand. He speaks in a dialect I don't get.

I can take this guy, my senses claim. I'm ready to begin.

I notice Babble and Guide have arrived. They've parked their bike's next to mine.

Now, the indistinguishable man says something I can clearly understand, 'This is not your place. Girlfriend and you run your mouth.'

Run my mouth? In context of what? You cannot be in on a story if you were not there. 'Girlfriend? Who is my girlfriend?' I raise my hands up, clearing the air in misunderstanding.

'Water girl, the slim one.'

He means Absentine.

'She is not my girlfriend.'

He smiles disapprovingly.

Babble and Guide are now at my side. Guide tries to walk me away, I untangle, half grin. I almost swear at the mustached potbelly man who allegedly sexual assaulted Absentine. My anger is palpable.

The potbelly man moves closer to the shorter man. The shorter man resists the potbelly man's hints to back away. He voices 'You leave now and never come back. You are not Simpatico. You are not Specialist. You will never be Simpatico. You drink designer tea you go to Studio. Whom do you think you are?'

Good, an answer to what this scene might be about. 'Invited Guest,' I smile. I haven't been to Studio other than to save Babble; I disregard that as Studio visit. How does he know I've drunk designer tea?

'Don't talk.' Guide instructs. 'Let's go, leave them be.'

I take Guide's advice begin to walk back to our bikes. No lounge tonight.

Simpatico allows this. Simpatico states a land without the threat of violence promotes unwelcome behavior worse than the brat that uses violence to solve problems. You may do whatever you like here. Punishment depends on the behavior. The potbelly man didn't say anything, no credit for this. Guilty. Maybe a start to his reform, I must consider.

We ride to the nearest open restaurant to eat.

Guide consults, 'What that man said is that designer tea is not a product on the market, why should you be drinking it. They also questioned what you are doing in Studio.'

I softly reply, 'That is not what it was about.'

It was all about Absentine, I think to myself.

Babble chimes. 'My fault, I was in Studio. I've been inquiring about designer tea. They must have us mixed-up,' Thankfully Babble confesses.

Guide responds, 'You observe you do not partake.'

How can I observe something I don't understand?

Nothing makes sense. Tourist Vacationer pay incredible fees to visit Studio, yet Visitor and Guest are chastised.

Guide instructs 'Protocol is followed that allows a Vacationer a holiday in Studio after legal papers are set. Designer tea is questionable in Simpatico. On a holiday it may be considered as a theme. Visitor, Guest, Specialists are here for a reason, not for mind displacement.'

'Always money,' comments Babble, as he'd spent a small fortune in Studio.

Guide, 'I don't know if you are doing a good job or not. Simpatico will answer that. Sometimes people will challenge you and we are okay with this. We will protect you if protection is warranted, provided you have stayed within your limits. Sometimes, in your job, you must cross the line safely. We cannot tell you to do wrong. It is unteachable like a dimension that isn't noticed. People in this world are often caught on one sphere; we are trying to change that. Go ahead and tread in the deep end, carefully.'

'Advanced human life not so advanced; we are still human ape.' I handle a fork.

'Maybe you're right, Lucky Ce,' grins Guide.

Grumbling done we say goodbyes. Guide goes back to wherever he lives. Babble and I discuss more of the commotion as we relax at Visitor Complex.

'I don't know. Ever since I've met Absentine things happen fast.'

Babble says, 'It is not Absentine, it is you. You are glowing because she is showing interest.'

I tell Babble of the hidden Absentine, a girl in a hut.

He is neither amused nor surprised. He's heard things, doesn't know things.

Absentine, when will we have contact? Sex without protection.

Gut me with a knife stupidity is my name. I love a puzzle. Absentine is a star to burn my life or grow it. My lust started all over, phase supreme. Seductive and wait.

'Life is great! You are Lucky Ce,' Babble grins.

Absentine is inward, traveling another galaxy, a lover of a thousand years. Doesn't mean we will ever be together. Master this universe to solve charts yet marked. Living in another dimension. I can't write it out, though I can write it a thousand times, a thousand ways. I think of her every day, every night, and it isn't just a thought; she appears with me inside out.

'I can have everything, live all my desires. And she can have hers because we have chemistry together.'

'Oh, fuck, slit your throat now.' Babble coughs, sick with my sounds.

I laugh at myself out loud. How ridiculous I sound. I like it. I like fun off-the-wall conversation.

No. Absentine can't break my heart. She gives power like no other. Not the same as a lover. A lover can kill my heart, bury it in the ground and I would never go back and dig that bleeding pump out.

'What about Chanel TV?' Babble reminds.

'Chanel is smart lust.'

We are happy, bullshitting out loud.

I thought in this age there is no violence, no torture, or abuse.

I have been confused. Naive.

Babble says I'm lucky Absentine does bring me to a higher power. He says I should have been beaten by the two men, yet I was only left to suffer words and warnings.

Late in the middle of the night I wake to write to Absentine:

'I feel your fire. Hot Woman — speak. Spiritual we travel, we meet. As physical humans where will we meet? If I need to decide, we'd meet near first, then Java, the volcano the ruins. Your bottom lip... magnificent, your delicate skin. When we said goodbye today the sun shone on only us while others froze. Inside our minds out through our vision, let the dead, the alive, the yet to be born view us. You think this is infatuation? You think this is fool? No. This is visibly invisible. Two powers, striking as one. Slowly I'm rising in flight with you.'

Her reply is. 'I agree.'

13

―――

IN THE FRESH MORNING air, I wave to her.

She waves back.

I follow her direction.

Chanel steps on my toes. 'I can show you something.'

What something?

'How's your girlfriend?'

Absentine, I can sense Chanel's brain.

'No girlfriend,' I play lost.

'The girl in the hut, Absentine?'

'I don't know.'

She moves close.

It's true, I can't resist her perfect everything. It's not fair, Absentine has no chance.

Chanel with her chin tilted up at me, we are almost kissing.

She doesn't break glance 'You want to know more about death in the astronaut chair now?'

'No.'

She giggles pushes me away, though she's the one made us close.

Her hands are tantalizing. She is tempting. It is good we are on the sidewalk of her store.

'What is Separation like?' I tempt.

'Simpatico, gives you freedom of choice. If you have a difference of opinion, stay here or go there. Making decisions is a learning of life. Live with the decision you make.'

'Maybe the same... here and there.'

'Maybe not. You have a simulation already as do I. A simulation here, also in Separation.

'I have a simulation?'

She takes my sentence from me, 'You might have never thought you'd make it this far. You agreed without agreeing. No big deal until you see a hilarious rendition of yourself.'

'Where do you see that?'

'Studio Port. North Villa, East Link. You haven't access,' she laughs. 'You must watch what you do in your life as it comes back to bite you. All the things that you think are embarrassing come out.'

She twists her arms around my shoulders bawling in chuckles, so funny.

'Come see me in the afternoon,'

'Okay.'

I greet Babble before he leaves on his bike.

Babble insanely happy with the thought of Chanel needing to show me something later today.

'You believe everything Chanel tells you? she confined and coerced you with sex,' he says jokingly.

'Seduced,' I appeal.

Babble and I at a standstill, almost giggling.

A notion an idea evolves — fractals.

A criminal can be a Simpatico citizen. A Bandit could be the most honest person. We haven't met any Bandits yet. They say the Bandit prefers to live in Separation. Not all Bandits came in illegally some are former Residents. Visitors have stayed on as Bandits, Specialist too, for whatever ill-gotten reason, for adventure, couldn't fit in, for no choice—become a Bandit.

Chanel in the afternoon.

'I have a room above the swimming pool. Let's go up.'

A walk, more near run.

'Wet my entire body, every hole. Suck me till I die.' Chanel at her worst best, 'I can't wait any longer.'

She does what I've thought of in Absentine.

Chanel, mind dream achiever.

My dream of Absentine seems implausible now. It is up to me to mess up this collaboration with Chanel. She speaks plain easy to my ears. Fits comfortable. Not dizzy, not circling Venus just standing on a Jupiter moon. Going well. This is not entrapment; check skyrocketing re-ignition.

We are a perfect ballet, breathing as meditating mavens.

'Finally,' she and I both say at the same time.

We don't roll away, we study high. Chanel studies me with a magnifying glass, laughing pleading to continue in her fun. The computer prints out their answers. Science is why she came in smiles. She is not an inventor. She came to test the inventions, worse than the wannabe prophet hailing outrageously, 'I think I'm smarter than everyone else. But I'm not.'

Thousands of Specialists work on any given day, inventing whatever they think they can be approved of.

She tells me to go deeper than Observer. I shake my head exhausted in her theories.

We both think we are more than we deserve. She goes, 'You are like a Specialist, you've been admitted because you can analyze and figure things out. Babble is your marketer.'

She walks to the bathroom and returns to the bed, adding, 'I input to the computer, though the computer is not needed. The computer is just my administrator. Everybody's admin is the computer. Humans really run the show. We input, and the computer outputs. If I say it is real, not everyone believes. If the computer says it real, it is to be.

She bites her finger. (Pause) 'I have a man. He is like a friend though. A sort of boyfriend.'

Where is she going with this? I've never asked her if she had a companion, nor cared.

'If he knew you were here, he'd go ballistic. He wouldn't leave me, I don't think. Not many choices here — short time sex sure this place has. My man be too embarrassed to have an affair on me. He'd go fuck someone, then he'd come back. Me, and you are here now tight as friends, unless we both fall in love. It will be short-lived our experience this afternoon and done again in time. What do you say?'

'You said it. We did it, and we may do it again.'

'You believe in first sight love. Spiritual molecule love. Everything I'm not. You don't know intellectual love, smart love. You know standing on the cliff broken-hearted love, dangerous love. Welcome to the new world Mr. Ce.'

'Okay.'

'You like the sex?'

'You are good. You make me good.'

'You aren't that good at it, Ce. But I'll take it, I'll take your emotions over skill. Skill can be learned.' She looks at me, her eyes glazed with glee, her lips waiting for laughter after my reactions... she's enamored.

I shrug.

She opens her mouth, neck stretched back, holding in giggles of her own jokes. Finally, I return her smile.

She goes on, 'What am I supposed to do when I already know. You are smarter than I am, in a different way. A way that can't be computed. Now you got it. Now you have your answer of why you have been deemed exceptional status — automatic Specialist.'

'Deemed by whom?'

'By me.'

'That's not real?'

'Oh, it's real.'

'Are you overriding the computer?'

'It is a fucking machine. Can it make itself?'

'Other machines manage it?' I consider.

'They are fucking machines. If you have the key, they can't lock you up.'

'You are worse than a machine.' I punctuate in sarcastic humor.

'I know. A machine is predictable. We tell the machine what to do. We are a long way from living two lives,' she laughs. 'One of you passes away... the other you alive. You experience both at the same time — alive and passing. The holiday vacations will be tricky. Technology, magic, and drug. Mindset. The perfect condition to experience death and yet still live. I'm not a scientist. Go speak to the scientist; they won't tell you. They've signed a contract. Some know some things and others know other things. Living in or with a computer, have all knowledge. Live forever. A body a brain transformed through AI. Some Residents don't care about that, they care about getting away from the world. Some were religious before, others never were. They want a release from this careless world. Simpatico cares about your dreams, it tries anyway. Like being on a ship, whether it's on the ocean or in the galaxies.'

'True, except you are still on Earth.'

'What is the Earth that we know. We adapt easily.'

'I better go.'

'You better. Say hi to Babble, tell him to forget about Scotch Cola — she likes to live half her life in a machine and half on designer tea.'

I return to the comfort of Visitor Complex. I don't check my messages.

Housekeeping, reception, kitchen, and maintenance staff at Visitor Complex are non-resident servers coming in for the day, weeks, or months, and then back to wherever they came from. Simpatico is popular for employment. Visitors flock to fill the positions offered.

14

———

BABBLE PLEASANT, AND I'm at peace.

Babble cares to inquire about designing a well-being drink with a hint of designer tea. Custom made for each consumer.

He's been in contact with a non-resident mixologist who specializes in mind-health enhancing concoctions.

Reminds me of the original Coca-Cola before cocaine was a deleted ingredient.

'Don't mention the profit part of it, just the idea to Chanel, you know how Simpatico thinks.'

To Star Natural.

Before Babble can even delve into his idea, Chanel interrupts us. 'Simpatico is sending you on a trip to nothingness in no-man's-land. You guys deserve a holiday.'

We are on a holiday — Babble thinks the same as I.

We agree to the trip. By early afternoon we are in East Link. Ushered into an underground building.

Servers guide us through a mediation process. We lie sedated in capsules resembling astronaut chairs. Length of stay yet to be determined. We experience noise, flashes of light, massaging sensations on our heads, pulsating vibrations on our muscles

— relaxing. Disorientated as we arise from the capsule. Our handlers don't say much. Carry on with instruction... drink the unknown.

The server calls it 'Potion tea.'

We are instructed to enter one door then exit another to no-man's-land. A server advises, 'If you can see the fence, you are not lost.'

A washroom break... then on with it.

We've been gifted knapsacks — containing water, an extra shirt, small blanket, towel, first aid kit, soap, and energy bars. The knapsacks also have a Simpatico location tracker.

Walk a long hallway through an automatic doorway to open natural light.

We follow a meshed open-air fenced walkway for a hundred meters. A gate closes behind us. Open landscape in front of us.

We are outside the fence of Simpatico. The caged fence secures itself to block the entrance back to East Link. We look dead (to) at each other.

Options: Hike it to the airport directly east, clearest route.

Slog to South Gate, farthest option.

Walk north to East Link entrance is the nearest, though we haven't access. We'd still need to hitch a ride on the looping road to the airport and beyond.

A service road is straight ahead... a ten-minute walk of wild terrain. Beyond is the airport, hills and bush. The service road intercepts the main road to the airport, South Gate, and town.

From the airport we can find transportation to South Gate.

We agree if lost or separated to wait at the airport, alternatively meet at a travel hut near South Gate.

Our trek begins to the airport. As where else would two aliens want to walk to? Earth is a playground — and Babble and I are cosmonauts. We have much serious work to do, this is our mind set.

We cross the service road, forge our own trail through the brush.

After ten minutes, feeling bewildered. Realm —surreal. I stop hiking for a few moments.

Babble hikes farther ahead up an incline.

Ripples, vibrations of my complete nothingness become the drama of life. No noise of Earth, no pumping heart. Just a vacuum sound that can be lightly heard.

I feel nervous, frightened to walk farther towards the airport.

The last instruction I remember was that if we stay in view of the Simpatico fence 'you won't get lost'. I'd forgotten this lesson. I cannot view the fence.

A change of direction, find a path that certainly directs me to the gravel ridden service-road I've traveled many times in the past. Unknown if Babble follows, I turn back to see if he is following.

I hear Babble chanting a howl.

My eyes see him standing at the top of an incline. He steps to the edge and tumbles down the hill, rolling as a child. Except Babble isn't playing.

Looks sore, painful at the bottom of the hill.

He stands up, does not dust himself off. He enters a running sprint. Howling loud with his hand to his mouth accentuating the sound.

Babble gone. Running away from humanity. Direction says he is headed southeast.

His vision strong enough to navigate through wilderness.

I tempt to follow slowly until phased with nothingness and stop following his direction. No longer standing on ground, no human body — I'm particles floating. Comfortably floating in a waterless ocean with no sight.

My thoughts aren't of blood flowing and breathing, my thoughts are of pure calm frightening elation. A reckoning. A controlled state amidst terror, much like in a fight when emotions and anger are subdued while positivity is commanding.

What will it be like to zoom down from this height — is a shocking thought.

Intuitively I change direction back the way I came. I wrestle back to humanity, feet on the ground, eyes visioning correctly. I cross the service road and see the fence of Simpatico in the distance.

Near the fence I feel most normal. I miss the unearthly exuberance of nothingness. I turn back towards the service road.

Not knowing how much time has elapsed. Seems like an hour stacked in minutes. I blink my eyes and here I am standing on a nonempty service road as two trucks raise dust in the distance.

I attempt a challenge and veer off the road into wilderness away from Simpatico.

Startled again by a soft vacuum sound that takes away what I've always known. Emptiness, my mind awash. I pull back to humanity.

Calm again, I'm walking south on a trail between the road and fence.

I can make my way to South Gate in an hour and half, I hope.

Fucking — Absentine, her essence feels strong. I walk the road with her enhancing my mind and body. With her confidence I walk off the road along a path in view of the fence. I walk in-between nothingness and normalcy. Viewing the fence is enjoying a state of shocked wellbeing. The closer the fence the more normal I feel. I find a medium best in-between the sound of nothingness and the natural sound of the world I've lived. I feel good. Slight nothingness is more enjoyable than normal.

It occurs I've also lived-in nothingness.

I see a cluster of travel huts and tents near the service road. They are inhabited. I don't stop to say hi, I ignore. Continue walking with purpose.

The busy main airport road is in the distance.

I follow a trail to the travel huts near South Gate where we'd agreed to meet as a last resort. Good thing a couple of them are unoccupied.

Communicating with security at South Gate is out of the question. Communicating with anyone other than Babble seems extreme and complicated as others seem a simple species while I consider myself an advanced being.

I twist open the water container tap, refresh, rest. I'm not lonely I'm particles in the universes.

To think is to travel to a destination. If there is a destination or if it is only modeled in the mind... I don't know. When focused the brain works at warp speed, we travel barely taking steps.

Time is the matter the brain needs to create the scene that was flashed by the mind.

I do not think about looking for Babble. Not a good time to experiment outside. I know Babble, he'll find his way. Possible he made it to the airport. He can accept a shuttle to South Gate, as planned.

I lie down close my eyes for what seems over an hour in wonder.

Footsteps on the outside of the hut.

Babble.

He has tree spines, sagebrush, and cactus needles sticking clinging to his clothing and skin. Dust in his hair, dirt on his person — he's a mess.

Speaks crazy... lost in no-man's-land. He'd thrown away his travel knapsack, didn't want to be location tracked. Later he went back and recovered the knapsack.

I want to laugh he's been lost wandering in nothingness, not knowing left or right. Walking circles, he thinks. Only Babble could do this, explore some sort of truth or fail for knowledge, for curiosity. For humanity, I don't think so. A man for his own reasoning goes and tries. This is the way humanity learns. Shocking stares of a man who just traveled from the center to the edge of a cell he'd never thought existed.

We decide to walk to the main road and hitchhike to town. Babble doesn't want to enter South Gate in his condition.

We are fortunate. A friend stops on the road — his name is Dutch. His property borders Simpatico. A familiar face we'd visit with Dutch daily during construction.

We should ask him a million questions; we only ask if he can drive us to town.

We answer his questions polite in single sentences. Comfortable in the position of passengers despite our exhausted condition.

Dutch laughs at us –– 'You drank too much Potion tea. Nothingness is what happens when you drink too much Potion. Lost in exhilaration, the only reprieve is comfort. Mommy...

Daddy,' his mouth boisterous nearly hooting. He calms down, 'You know, I've been offered a lot of money for my property.'

Sell.

'Too much fun here to sell... especially with guests like you two.'

Babble fake chuckles.

Dutch comforts, 'Listen, Simpatico is working on a bunch of shit. I don't know all the terminology, but they are not going to be experimenting on you two. You'll be fine in the morning.'

Fun has no limits. Smiling shine of the moon.

If you believe in God, I'm placed here.

If you believe in Gods, I'm lead here.

Evolution, I belong here.

Computer simulated, engineered here.

Alien, I'm studied here.

I believe in none of that.

Bohemian obscure.

Check into the hotel, sleep.

In some ways I would rather have rolled down a dirt hill, fall in cactus and shrubs, be addicted to death experience than what I have fallen — fallen to lust of a Simpatico woman. Babble's misgivings easily dissolved in the brain. Mine are full chasing.

Imagine if the world was watching. His scene is funny, mine insane.

In simulation Simpatico watches, Residents watch, Scientist watch. In some simulations you can watch another person's every move, and they can observe yours. Residents feel at first uncomfortable but after seeing others, like in a family home you get used to it and soon you stop minding.

In the morning, I call my wife. Health fine — some good news some bad news, regular talk.

After breakfast Babble and I order a taxi. Begin our way back to Simpatico.

Babble pleasant, I'm at peace. We agree to meet up discuss with Chanel TV after we relax in our rooms. We rest for the whole day. Nothingness is exhausting.

Hype about Simpatico experience exceeds truth, more devastating than advertised. In Society commercial advertisements usually overpromise, and the product seldom matches the result. In this utopia commercial advertising understated, and the product exceeds expectations.

15

A SIGNAL PROGRAMMED to our minds. Enhanced brain. Alter dimension, too much exaggeration. Or click, undetectable audio?

The sound wave of nothingness — a clever frequency.

Star Natural to debrief.

We find out Potion tea is a name given to a type of designer tea.

I, Babble, Chanel, plus her co-server sit as a group smiling, thinking humorously about walking in no-man's-land.

'You know how a dog can hear a signal and a human can't. They can detect sounds we can't hear, right?' Babble says.

'Our brains have access to a no-man's-land frequency. Clicking as we wait for connection to another world. They are using no-man's-land as a border, except on the road to town, the airport, and near the fence. Everything else in the territory is nothingness, no-man's-land,' says Chanel's co-server.

'How?' We all wonder.

A signal to our minds, subliminal messaging, drugged? Game station! We laugh together.

'Woooo!!!!' Glad. None of us have answers.

Chanel informs us that before the fence was built Residents would inform security, enter capsule, drink Potion tea, wander in no-man's-land until they experienced nothingness. Return home and reflect on it.

'No astronaut chair,' I comment.

'We have always had a capsule and astronaut chair. They have been upgrading every year.'

'Perfect security — Residents never leave.' Chanel's co-server remarks.

Though Babble and I did leave until the next day.

'You are non-residents,' is Chanel TV's claim.

'Travelers aren't distressed by nothingness in no-man's-land.'

'Nope.'

Babble leaves. He gets no clear direction in pursuit of his well-being drink from Chanel TV. She has no interest in discussing it. Her co-server moves into a small cubical with a computer.

Chanel does not partake in Potion tea. 'Only once. Just because you can try drugs in Amsterdam, see a psychiatrist in LA, or be sabotaged by audio in Cuba, doesn't mean one wants to.' Pause. 'Mind manipulation? Not my thing. It's all perception creation. Simpatico likes to claim it is working on a system, a signal, a wave, a tremor, a vacuum etc. I'm not sure what it is. The idea is that a frequency triggers the events you experience. Signal security in the case of no-man's-land. But that is just an example it is more than that. They are working on a signal that creates your perception — models your brain to its perception. Maybe Alien intelligence has been using this on us for thousands of years, and we are just learning it. If a signal can manipulate us to stay close to Simpatico, I imagine it can manipulate choice and catastrophes. I don't even know what's real, if they use a signal or just tell us they use a signal, and we obey.'

'Uh.'

'Get it?'

'Got it. Alien technology. The answer to why we can't do things we desperately want. An unseen force rules our existence. Pain suffering joy and celebration if you test the limits of yes and no. Or perhaps no technical advanced system at all, just our minds from here to the never-ending sky.'

'Think as you like. But I'll tell you if you went for a walk outside today, you'd feel nothing — just another normal day.'

'Did they build the travel huts for Potion tea takers, a place to feel safe, hid out, rest?'

'I don't know. The computer says build them, or a person tells the computer to build them. Servers build. Take care of the not haves and have-nots.'

Customers enter her store. Her co-server takes care of the customers. Chanel walks me out.

'You must come to Studio with me at the end of the week. Promise. I have the Studio booked for a couple of days.'

'Yes,' to Studio.

Perhaps nothingness is all in the mind perpetrated by Potion tea, and no technology at all. Or perhaps the Potion tea is intelligent; technology so advanced it alien. A little of both, I imagine. Maybe there is an undetectable signal helping our choice in decisions. Maybe nothing at all. Suggestion is all.

Chanel TV, you've sparked my brain.

'Write a book.' Her last words.

An experiment doesn't always agree with the passion you hoped to suffer. Sometimes you get caught up, stuck in destructive behavior, a depression, it isn't all mountains and plains.

I haven't checked messages or contacted Absentine for days. I've been playing some kind of — "look I'm cool game" that I can stay away from her, though I can't.

16

―――

YESTERDAY IN DELIGHT.

Today plunged with a knife.

I guess I didn't write her a verse every day.

Poetry seemed kind of silly... actually.

Absentine is to be married.

She'd sent a message the day before yesterday.

Her message — 'I'm to be married soon.'

I use a Simpatico phone at Visitor Communication Centre to respond.

What's going on, is the best I can do.

Her words. 'You are happily married. I'm to marry someone too. I have met someone I want to spend some of my life with. He's asked me to marry. I said yes. Why not?'

I cannot answer a symbolic question, not in the mood. I'm not crushed.

I say good luck, wish the best, hope marriage works for you.

All my lying love.

She makes the sound of a cat... then tears up 'Say goodbye before I change my mind.'

I will never say goodbye.

She's leaving Simpatico on a marriage holiday. There is no such thing as marriage ceremony in Simpatico. She will be married to a Specialist who works in both Separation and Simpatico. They've known each other since before Simpatico Separated.

Hanged to dry is I.

For some reason Absentine and I exist in another dimension where we can succeed. My life seemed glorious. I couldn't find a stream of collapse. Absentine always a near surrounding entity.

Spiritual lover you are one of a kind.

She has her dream. Death to the mystic, death to the goddess. I am plain. Simple. Science and universe.

Simpatico, I realize is a release from this Godless Earth.

I'd cheated on her love, why shouldn't she cheat on mine? Fine she can have her marriage, I'm not racing inside.

I dismiss her marriage talk. Dismiss her unreliable love for another man. She's made her own mistake. I won't be the one she hates. I support her happiness, not willing to falsely state, 'Don't marry, I love you.' She can fail on her own. I think perfect we can be lovers. No risk for family, wife, pregnancy, money, and all that comes with a relationship.

She's gone her way.

Absentine, I thought you liked women, and I had no competition. I was wrong.

Handcuffed. A wife I can't see and a woman I can't touch.

Simpatico will murder. Simpatico will vanquish. Simpatico will punish. Still, I lust you.

Pregnant now! Her belly full. Yes... I've said it, I want her pregnant. She can have her marriage to fail. I will have her pregnant with my child.

As evil as they come. Destroy everything I've built or add to it. Two thoughts collide... create one.

If I have her when she is pregnant or if I make her pregnant it doesn't matter. I see her belly pregnant.

Absentine! I yell her name happy I've survived.

In a trance, I begin to ride my bike.

Babble and I have dinner together like we do most evenings.

I think out loud, 'The ultimate solution: To experience death to be dead and to live as well. Two of you — the living you and the dead you. I don't understand the four in Simpatico. Is that four? Living in this reality, living simulated, simulated and reality together as an advanced being is only three. What is the four in Simpatico?'

'Living, simulated, dead, and all together as a techno advanced human alive and dead, that's four.' Babble comments not missing a chew of his meal. He's thought this answer before.

'I don't know if that makes sense.'

'Four doesn't make sense Lucky,' as in none of it makes sense.

Babble and I funny, screaming snickers of the confusing hilariousness of Simpatico.

'You want to hear about Absentine,' I look at Babble.

'Always back to Absentine,' Babble punctuates.

'She's left Simpatico to be married to a Specialist working in both Separation, Simpatico, and Society at times.'

Babble grins kind, 'She will be married as much as you are married. So be it. She may have loved you more than you loved her. She knew she could never be with you.'

My mind circles.

'Stop thinking about Absentine. Did you make a promise a plan together?' Babble questions.

'No, just hints.'

'Exactly. You were never with her. That's a fact.'

'Yes, maybe.'

'We live as Gods here.'

'You can't say "God".'

'Ha-ha oh yeah. We walked in and experienced everything grand. And now you want to engage greed? You have a million.

I want my million, and I don't mean in investment. I want a million in cash at my dispense, real money. Everyone is rich with property or business. I want disposable cash. Crazy free.'

Babble has given up on his thick girl, fire went out. The hottest don't burn slow. Scotch Cola too, he's slowly forgotten. Scotch Cola is never around, missing, not heard from. He's in a state to prove he's here for more than fun. He seems disgruntled.

'What is wrong with you?' A friendly request.

'Nothing,' Babble pretends before truth. 'I want it all: Separation, Society, to die and live again. The four as Chanel says. Plus, I want money to spend back home, do as I please. What about you?'

'I don't know... maybe die and live at the same time would be nice. I'll take the two — a life here and my life in Society.'

'That makes four' Babbles corrects.

Back to me, 'Life is about in-between the numbers. Mathematics is the easy solution. What happens in-between, Babble?'

'Nothingness. No-man's-land. A system to school the children to pass myth as knowledge for generations.'

'Just like home. Afraid of things we have no proof. Stories become more extreme than truth. We are here for our fantasies, the ones we don't want to admit. My millions can wait, I guess. People pay a million for a vacation in Simpatico. I sound poor.'

'You are, and so am I. But today for this short time we are rich. We are both rich when compared to the poor, and poor compared to the rich. We are poor rich, living as the privileged for another nine days.'

It is true we are coming to the end of our contract.

Babble determined we should develop a designer tea well-being drink of our own.

I hesitate — I don't say yes, I don't say no, let it play. It would be on the up and up, nothing funny, just drinks to your own liking. Personalized cognitive drinks mixed with a weakened designer tea.

We sleep on that.

17

THEY SET YOUR BODY temperature at such a rate your vital signs react — you think you are dying, dead. Simpatico is the medicine man, the travelling salesman.

The death of man has no strings.

At first nothing appeared until in a second everything appeared.

The two factor, live die, separation.

To be one with technology. To be one with nature. Internal External. To be content in any surrounding.

Computer, natural. Simulated, death. Keep measuring for infinity in theory.

Achieve insight from this woman with a smile as stunning as the days sun. She is the seducer. She clung to me, her dirty blonde hair, her vanishing sunburn does not belong to me.

"Come on in"

When I walk into her reserved Studio, there is nothing, empty space.

Just a mat. A bowl, a piece of fruit, a vegetable on a shelf of the wall. No computer simulation system, no capsule, no astronaut chair, no television, I see a small music system and a dozen of books.

She is advanced, not one with machine.

She has ventured into my dreams.

'This is my design! I gutted it,' she exclaims.

I'm understanding "Studio" is the word for the entire space — capsule area is where magic happens.

Chanel knows she doesn't need to waste time on a designer tea, a simulation system, a theme room in capsule, or on an astronaut chair, she can live a designed life naturally; she's that brave.

'You want a drink of water?'

Okay.

She walks close offers a sip as she holds the glass to my lips. 'I won't seduce you this time.' Poker-Faced. She places the glass of water to the floor, turns smiles and sits down on the mat.

She hasn't a chance. My turn.

Lion.

I kneel, draw my arms around her from behind. Classic, she gives up her neck.

My hands do what they are instinctually told. Wander slowly to her zones.

It isn't long before we are having relations half on half off the mat. We edge to every corner of the room. Positions made up, twisted bent. I try to hold one last breath.

She is pretty. Now what will I do?

I cannot stay.

I cannot stay with her. She would tie me up, stroke me, challenge me with other lovers. She is the kindest evil as the world has understood. The evil of kindness that man dreams, break you down, you slap her, and she never concedes.

She is advanced human, she needn't a thing. She tells, 'Once you commit to belief, you become Simpatico.' She walks in pace turns, 'You are on the cusp, but you are only venturing you are not committing.'

If technology advances life, you must also experience death. 'What about born?' I ask.

'Born is always. You don't know it is happening except others can see it.'

I should be telling her about life, not her telling me.

I tempt her, 'In death you know what's happening, others can't see it.'

Silence. No touching.

'You don't have to leave. You have no obligations today; you are in Studio.' She sighs.

No bed, she puts a blanket down on the floor with four pillows.

I guess I'm staying. Truth I've been waiting for this. This is why I came.

We make love late in the night — sideways slowly in maximum dance, glued together in passion. We are combined sweat: knees, forehead, hip, toes, nose.

Now I want to slurp a bowl of soup.

After all the underlying reasons, I have my answers. This afternoon, this morning, I've slept in the Simpatico Studio. Nothing like I expected. I have accepted death. Healthy in life. Be simpatico with pain, joy, wealth, and deprived. Accept wisdom, right or wrong. Do your life's work. One with technology, one with life and death; experience all. Advance to the beginning. Die at the start.

How many days can I stay as is?

I didn't expect anything today or yesterday. I expected nothing — I thought maybe science fiction, a game, virtual reality, sleep in a chamber, a coma. What I have is exactly what I want: luscious babe, back it up, start again all day. Advanced life?

It is true we are no secret relationship now. We embrace on the sidewalk of East Link.

The first drizzle of rain I've seen.

It rains on the planet I live on.

Rain is no problem; you know why it rains. You know there are many planets like ours... still this is not why you want to cry.

You want to cry the unknown.

We walk through a park. Restaurant for lunch. Tired now.

Chanel waiting for me to argue, give her something.

She knows what I like. Takes away what I like.

She tells, 'You must understand when you die the simulation continues. And if you are brought back to life you will engage in this life. In a simulation I'm a skater, a figure skating teacher. Not married, looking for someone. Sometimes I go back and see how I'm doing. Simulation makes sense. Real life doesn't.'

She waits momentarily before speaking more. 'Fractal. Nobody likes the truth.' She turns away, 'I'm having an affair in simulation.'

'An affair with whom?'

'With you.'

'Really?'

'I'm stealing you away from the simulated woman who is trying to have your baby.'

'Who is trying to have my baby?'

'Absentine.'

Did she just say Absentine?

I try to ignore what she said. 'How is a baby born in simulation?' I query.

'It isn't. You physically do it. I don't know why she wants you. The gene pool is small in Simpatico. The best ones are taken by the best ones. That leaves her with you.'

I don't even laugh, though I'm sure it's outrageously funny. 'What are you saying?'

'I'm saying, you're great and all that but....'

'But what?'

'It will be a fatherless child. Suppose that's what she wants. She must look at her pluses mixed with your minuses, and vice versa, and say "Yeah, I might even enjoy fucking him too". Chanel loving her explanation.

'You think?'

'She knows you'd enjoy it. She knows you'd jump her and neglect perfections because you are chasing her, and she's letting you chase. You won't even know what hit you... a baby!' Chanel slaps my leg.

'Maybe I can't have children?'

'Oh yes, you can, or at least have the chance. You've been tested; she knows that. Portal knows lots about you, it has your blood sample... it can get your sperm too.'

She grasps my face, says a verse in French, squeezes my cheeks, and kisses my lips. 'I'm not pregnant yet.' She exclaims. 'Bahahaha!!!!' She is so funny. 'We in Portal have been asked to study our lives. That is our responsibility. We need children to begin inputting life events to Portal from the beginning. Children need to be raised in Simpatico from the beginning. A child born of a new culture. A huge obligation for a parent.'

'Will you have a child?'

'I have Simpatico if I want a father for my child. I'm thinking about it. Let's say I'm analyzing the situation. I have a year or so left to think before I do. So yes, have fun now.'

We go to her store. Fire up her Portal. See what's new.

I still haven't asked about the comments she made of Absentine. I think she was clearly joking of an underlying truth.

'Babble is already in Separation,' she thrills.

'How do you know?'

'In the system. He may never be able to leave. Go get your things. I'm sending you to Atmosphere maybe you'll find your Absentine as well. I know you love her.'

'Yeah right... love.' I shrug her off.

'Absentine could have seen you whenever she liked, she was not ready or is not ready. She does not want a man from Society. Heartbroken. She does not want to be a deserter. Simpatico is her home.'

'She married a non-resident, a Specialist. She went to Society to be married.'

'Yes, I know. She hasn't gone through with the marriage. She only promised him "a maybe". Marriage is nothing here, that won't stop someone from seeing another.'

Good to hear.

'Why do you and Scotch Cola hate on Absentine?'

'Scotch Cola only knows things from chemical experiments created in the body with the help of technology. She looks down on Absentine. Absentine doesn't need technology or chemical enhancement. Absentine tries to create uniqueness without any artificial enhancement just the natural abundance in her heightened being.'

Chanel knows Absentine — they've interacted in Star Natural. Absentine trained as a chef at Relax Lounge where Scotch Cola serves. All three together in sports activity.

Women.

Chanel adds, 'People in Simpatico don't act like they did in Society. We are civil. Perhaps in simulation not so much.'

I'm to leave tomorrow before noon for Atmosphere.

I leave Chanel and go gather, pack up my belongings from Visitor Complex.

Front desk says Babble has checked out.

At communication center a message from Babble: 'See you on the other side (Separation) or when I return. I had to move fast. Later my friend!'

I place my luggage in storage, next to Babble's. I park my bike next to Babble's and leave the keys at the reception desk.

Imagine... Babble and I are still looking for more taste of it (Simpatico). We both feel we are just at the appetizer. Now we are both headed for Separation.

Choices: up, down, left, right, or stay the same plane. If all is good, stay on projection. If, and when blasé hits, try another direction.

Maybe run into another like Absentine. The greatest gift the greatest moment — never tasted, never understood.

I know you fall in love before you make love. Making love only confirms it. Intensifies it.

Sleep.

In the morning, I walk over to a supply store next to Visitor Complex before I'm to make my way to East Link.

18

MY COMPUTER BRAIN RUNS slow when I'm very tired.

Pixilated moments focus, to gorgeous.

A uniquely specialized woman I've visualized before. Guaranteed happy.

Absentine gleaming.

To be fair I thought I may never see her again.

I wait for her to move first, pleasant. A companion transverse the earth. I'm loyal. Fun has no limits. Smiling shine of the sun.

I like her fashion for the first time, she excels. Makeup and stature. She is stunning it is true.

It is also the first time I've seen her daughter. I realize her daughter has a near original mind, having come to Simpatico at the age of five.

They are exiting the supply store.

'Where have you been?' Absentine's eyes scream.

She is not completely happy — her body language tells.

Absentine shakes her head slightly in disappointment, 'Relationships are hard work.'

I complicate things: 'It is what you wanted.'

'What you want isn't always what you get.'

It was all a dream she is a normal human, weak. I cared to tender her.

'Message me,' Absentine breaths positive as they proceed to a remote shuttle van.

'I'll message you.' I stare at her cheeks as she walks away.

Two energies creating solo paths to discover destiny. Here we are separating. I have not made a mistake, even if we are just friends. Gone from intergalactic eyes I instantly begin to formulate what message I will send. Then I remember I may no longer be able to send messages from Atmosphere side of Simpatico to her.

It occurs to me, she never married; she is free to be with me, and I'll be gone. I didn't even ask if she is single now. Never mind, it will be better as a surprise when I return.

Will this rid my love for Absentine? Perhaps intensify it.

I have the sun I have the moon I have pleasure that warmth, cold, and wind are meant to give. If I cannot voluntarily suffer, be ridiculed, wade in the waters of trouble, and live undesirable, how can I attain the highest desirable.

Live simple, alone in the forest, in the desert, in the mountains, or on the plains. Live simple first or live simple second, doesn't matter. Simple before living well or live well before humble.

Learn to suffer brings about best.

Charmed our whole life, some kind of question will be asked. Live well volunteer mad before tortured. Inside our unknown takes us towards dreadful. Humiliation brings strength, resolve, never to be repeated. Charmed life, a calm that will not bring great change, a rock that does not roll. Steady is good. Steady is not sculpted, steady is not revered, steady is not challenged. If you want to go higher, you need unsteady. You need to fall.

Give me fail at simple. Give me success at difficult.

In simple English, it's great to experience being in love with somebody.

Whatever you do to succeed you must close everything else off.

Brunch at a secluded table, East Link lunch inn. Waiting for my entry pass to Separation side.

Chanel assures me, 'You are an Observer. Information approved, no secrets. The governments, other companies are thought out by Simpatico. Simpatico figures out whom will leave Simpatico and start their own company. Simpatico feeds the double crosser, the quitter, the spy, and false information until they are gone. If Portal can't figure it out, a dependable man is hired to figure it out. Simpatico considers you responsible to deliver Simpatico stories to the world. A free man, like the world should be.'

'Babble was hired by Simpatico as an Observer... but why, why Babble?'

'Babble was a calculated decision; if wrong there is a reason.'

I rest, I have no more questions. Only a truth.

'I saw Absentine this morning.'

Chanel hesitant... 'Nobody knows if she is brilliant or ridiculous. No one can figure it out.'

'She has the most incredible out-of-this-world energy as any person I've met.' A sober admittance of how much I've decided on Absentine.

'You have answered your own question; she has something I don't.'

'She can't compete with you.'

'That is why she is so bothersome — because she doesn't have to compete. I have nothing against her. You and I are not about her. You are mixed with morals. Those morals exposed on the walking ground create a spiritual world, just like her. No wonder she wanted a baby making love to you.'

I forget to laugh. I'm confounded. Is what she says about Absentine true?

Chanel's head down. 'Create something out of thin air. Like Absentine and you. All a mindset. Simpatico presents the Resident with a dream.'

'Did Portal tell you to seduce me?'

'Yes, the computer told me to roll on the floor with you, slap your ass.' She laughs. 'No.'

We are smarter than the computer. Humans go against everything that says no. We are unpredictable. Humans can behave in ways that another human detests, like an infected computer. A human recording every minute of their life and then reacts. Can the computer replicate this? It can, I think. But it cannot predict the random the unknown quality of a human.

Chanel settles to seriousness, 'It is difficult to figure out life. You must start when you are a child. I can tell you to start this year, but bad karma can last twenty years and what happened today you may not be able to date back twenty years. You can try and start today though it won't be exact because you can't examine your entire life. I mean you could. You do, but you haven't input the calculations. Write and calculate all that has happened, use numbered events and figure out what your life means, predict the future.'

'A true practitioner.'

'If you figure out actions, add them, minus them, you can predict.'

'Counting sins.'

'Kind of, though not fucked up like popular religion. Not make believe. Get all that you have been taught out of your head.'

'I see. Will you input this interaction to Portal?'

'Yes. I want to see the results — plus or minus... fucking with you.'

'That was only fucking?' I speculate.

'You thought making love, soul mating?'

'Not at first but once in the action, maybe.'

'It was good. I knew it would be because I chart my life. You were predicted. First time resistance... second time enjoy, third time comfortable, fourth freedom. There will be no fifth time with us. There is nowhere to go. No up down left or right — only dissolve. I'm leaving on a trip.'

'Enjoy.'

'Will you write about me?' she looks to me.

'I don't think so. Just parts.'

'Not in love with me?'

'I don't have to be in love to write. Something comes out or doesn't.'

'Is that what you think?' She won't give up.

'It isn't what I think, it is what I know.'

'God doesn't scare... because it has all the answers for you, protects you. God reins you in, corrects you until you are solvent. God can be whatever you like, and no God can be whatever you like because it is your world inside your mind. A God through Portal is a God that really does answer. I don't know why I talk about God or Gods; it is stupid thinking. It is ancient. We only discuss it for comedy — like "how stupid can you be". The trouble with the world in one sweep is Gods thinking.'

Chanel TV calculates the landing of all possibilities, the worst disaster the best scenario risk reward.

She is matter of fact. 'You are in love with your wife. You won't leave her.'

We say goodbye.

What I decipher from Chanel is that Absentine and I are affectionate in a simulated world. Does Absentine know this? She must.

Chanel said there will be no fifth time romantically with her. Once in her store, once above the pool, twice in Studio — that's her four.

I consider we can make love, one more time in some place new — that's my four.

19

IN SIMPATICO — SIMULATION happens in a hundred different experiments. One day you're a hero, the next a fake, and ultimately fall, as we all do.

An advanced human — a fusion of technology and human traits — stands in contradiction to both Absentine and Chanel. They have been accepted by Simpatico, yet their ideals seem natural. Perhaps technology is the most natural non-living thing.

Chanel and Absentine will use technology to advance to the natural hidden world they see, like a saw to cut wood to build a house faster. Technology, a tool to cut through dimensional space quicker than waiting slowly through ages.

The richest, advanced, brilliant, experimental — and possible wrong. Simpatico.

I understand in Separation you can add to the projection of life, or you can just Serve. You can study, watch, be entertained, or participate, create. One thing is certain: once in Simpatico this side or Separation side your life is simulated as a projection. You are part of technology.

Simpatico offers all possibilities of what life can be. Learn the unknown, the undiscovered. Peace to survive in any current state. Die and then make your choice. Experience death and live forever. A complete cell.

I leave for Separation, travel underground.

Enter a Portal Booth to East Link Free Zone. Follow instructions. I'm given entry code to a waiting room.

Wait three hours. Refreshments. A screen projecting Simulated world can be looked, I look, but I haven't recognized anybody in the scenes of the Simulated world. Yes, I'm anticipating and fearing a recognition of self.

The entry door opens, leading to the underground transport tunnel from East Link to Separation, I presume.

A passenger travel van is parked at the beginning of the tunnel roadway.

I walk towards the van as a man in the driver's seat waves me over.

The driver instructs, 'Gather your things together in the back seat, the rest of your luggage is there. Hop in.'

All my luggage previously stored at Visitor Complex has been preloaded into the van.

We drive through the tunnel. A metal gate closes behind us. We drive into sunlight.

Feels familiar, looks familiar, is familiar.

Well... I've been separated. I'm not dead. Just outside the Simpatico boundary.

The van slowly rolls over a bumpy section before accepting the smooth road to the airport.

'To town, sir?' The driver asks.

'To town. Presuming I can't return to Simpatico.'

'No sir, you have been released. Your contract expired.'

Past the airport we drive to South Gate.

The van stops.

'Sir, we must wait for another passenger.'

Babble I presume.

Not Babble, not a person I know. We drive to town.

'Where do you want to be dropped off at, sir?'

'Hotel' same as before.

I don't ask him why I've been released.

The driver has an answer, though, 'You never know why. Like death, it just happens.'

I wasn't searched nor my luggage inspected with contraband detectors. I'd stashed designer tea in the luggage. The system defeated itself.

Bring me peace.

There are three of you: The good, the bad, and the in-between.

The fourth of you is the unknown.

I'm in a temper, in a pattern I'm not to destroy anything. I'm going home. The poor travel the rich travel. Most vacation. To travel you barely have shoes on as you set off for life or death.

My hands reach to the stars then clasped down before up to the sky again.

I've stopped kissing my clasped hands as Absentine does. I've found my own breathing pose technic. True, I follow her initial direction.

Home

I'm no longer a millionaire.

I'm not broke, certain of that. Dreamed a million and dropped to half like that. Investment gone wrong — however you want to classify it, a lot of money gone. Wait again for the investments to rise — maybe a year, maybe five years, maybe never again.

Millionaire... I laugh at the word. Poor has time, rich has time; in the middle striving has no time.

Desire the joker.

Love family... feel free.

A week has passed since I left Simpatico.

Today I check my Email.

A message from Simpatico Portal:

'Come Lucky Ce. Have an opportunity for you. An opportunity that pays in experience, in valuables. Daily Favors for living expense. A bonus of converted Favors to your wallet at the end of the tenure of approximately two weeks.

Thank you for your perceived agreement to Serve.'

Date and travel arrangements are made.

I agree to return in twenty-eight days.

Babble's wife says he's stayed on exploring options for residency. She will ask Babble to contact me.

Contact with Absentine — nothing.

No contact with Chanel — maybe she was right, no fifth time.

Simpatico, one can hide. There should be a place on Earth where a person can hide

Entertain

―――

TO SAY THAT YOU ARE only tangible is nonsense. You can be in different forms of existence.

The most fascinating thing in life is the evolution of thought.

Did a computer build invent the universe? It is just a thought of where we are at, in what we can do now. Like when we first studied the stars or when we began to read and write, our next theory of discovery will permeate a new belief. We can only study what we know. We can't study what is beyond our realm.

Keep guessing what we are.

Your personal relationship with existence may not be the same as your brother or sister, so don't push them. Let them be in their relationship with their supreme ideas.

East Link

Store of Information.

An older woman wearing a white lab coat walks away from my eyes as I stand alone in Store of Information. I speak to a younger second woman about what kind of information is available at the store. She doesn't tell me; she asks questions instead. We both tell lies in laughing chatter. Our communication is intriguing, enjoyable. She seems somewhat attracted to me. I've forgotten what information I came in for — nothing really, just check out the store, ask about my friend Babble Skorn. We are interrupted by others seeking info. I leave the store.

I've been sequestered for two days for medical tests and orientation with no pass to leave this part of East Link. I can't even go to Relax Lounge and ask if Babble Skorn has been around.

If examination results are favorable, visiting Atmosphere is next, possibly tomorrow.

After a night's sleep, Store of Information in the morning.

Information hasn't a notice. Bothering her, the Greeter is the interest.

I cannot determine her age, she's possibly in her mid-thirties, at the height of her attractiveness.

Her name is Scena.

She is indescribable. Her hair is neither straight nor complete curly, not black nor brown, maybe it's dark red. Her stature is strong and her voice abstract, her legs thin.

'Oh... you like Store of Information.'

'I have come to ask about a friend.'

Six seconds of silence before she smiles. 'We don't offer that kind of information; find the information yourself. We only provide the means.' She is shockingly mysterious. 'You want to know the means?'

Still smiling Scena holds out a Favor scanner.

'Expensive?' I assume.

'Good value. Are you rich?'

'No' I retort, 'About you — are you rich?' politely back.

'I live here, run this store with my aunt. Yes, rich.'

I pass her a Favor receipt. She scans it to see if it fits.

'If you don't like it, don't come back. First time is free.'

I look at her puzzled. She hasn't given me anything.

'I owe you Favors,' she gleams. 'Go on an adventure find your friend is my advice.'

She hands me a drink in a sealed cup. It is designer tonic.

I shake my head no... 'I don't need it.'

I push the cup away.

She says 'Fine, so you're advanced.'

We laugh slightly.

'Soon I will leave,' I claim trying to end the conversation.

'And never come back?'

'I don't know. Maybe to see you.' I was thinking it, and now I've said it.

Scena firm, 'I'll come see you. Atmosphere, Studio Port?'

Well... this is working.

'Yes. Correct.' One or the other, I think.

Scena confident, 'I'll find you. I owe you a Favor.'

We leave it at that.

I can't wait any longer in East Link. I must make my way to Atmosphere territory at the end of the walk through a Portal Booth. My medical examination results good.

I read an explanation of Studio Port:

"You create a simulated existence. Sometimes you can be sleeping and continue with your creation like you'd slept in it. Soon you eat when and what you eat in the simulation. After a while you are living exactly like the simulation. When you take a break from simulation, it is like taking a break from life. As an example of break, take a walk. You must exercise a certain amount of time to power your electricity; otherwise, you can't resume your simulated life. Don't worry — the exercise part is modelled to your ability. Basically, you must work a little to have access. The set up for chores is modelled to your physical and mental abilities. Total health."

2

AUTUMN IN ATMOSPHERE.

The feel is unsettling. Maybe it is the weather, the heat gone.

I've checked into Discount Store, which has prearranged rooms for invitees and serves breakfast. Discount Store is where physical items arrive and leave from a warehouse next to the store.

Dusk, I check out the Atmosphere scene, stepping to the corner of Main Street undecided on direction.

'Where do you want to go?' A woman's voice in a safe harmonious tone, 'Left, or right?'

To the left are office buildings, apartments, and an empty lot as the street carries on towards East Link.

To the right, Station House, a restaurant, a shopping store as the street carries on to Advanced Experimentation.

The next street over is Studio Port.

'I want to go dancing,' I respond.

She laughs.

I turn to see her in the sparse light. I'd never have talked so bluntly if I'd known she was lovely.

'No dance hall here. I can show you a place.' She smiles, her dark hair slicing across strong cheekbones. An open jacket exposes a pleasant hip to shoulder physique.

We go right.

'Who are you?' I ask.

'I Serve Simpatico.'

We walk pleasant.

'You came here for what?' she asks.

'I've come to find a friend.'

'Where is your friend?'

'Maybe in Atmosphere.'

'Maybe in Studio Port,' she nods beyond the street towards Studio Port.

Names are not exchanged.

She takes my hand, 'We can dance in here.'

We enter a restaurant. She leads me to the back room, a few tables, poorly lit. Soft-music plays.

She faces me, moves close.

Dance.

Her arms around my neck strong, urging me down to her height. We kiss. An impossible kiss.

Exquisite kissing trembling of fatal afterthoughts. Kissing to lift me beyond humanity to a truth that can't exist.

I'm just telling you... she is the best.

Maybe I've found this kind of kissing expertise once, twice before.

We are just beyond the gaze of a few people at the nearest table. We dance slowly.

Our rhythm falters, as a displeased Manger approaches, 'Are you going to have something to eat?'

She indicts no.

'We better leave.' Takes my hand, walks me home.

In the light of my room, she is not perfect.

I gasp. 'Your eye?'

Her left eye is crooked. A small scar to the side of her eye socket is present.

She looks at me slowly shaking her head no, don't ask.

She kisses me until I forget the question.

The question I have is why so fast. And what happened to your left eye.

I fear to engage in this desire... too good to stop though.

She educates: 'You are a new face, exciting — you aren't like the regular guest. You spoke the right words — "Go dancing!"'

She manipulates my freedom, staring intensely with her right eye directing my attention to her pulse. Her left eye looking half at me.

Passion.

She is shirtless and I am pant less.

Tremendous.

She isn't exactly good, good would be someone more practiced with motions of habit — her sweetness is real.

We don't go too far. 'Too early for us,' she explains, before comforting, 'I will come see you again.'

'What's your name,' I ask.

'Crooked Eye.'

I can't just call her Crooked Eye, can I?

'It's okay — it was written. I was named "Crooked Eye" before I assumed the recognition.'

I accept her explanation. Don't ask questions.

Our experience ends as quickly as it starts. She leaves.

Her curves, her quiet storm have left me in a comfortable peace.

I sleep contentedly only to be woken by a call to my room from the reception of Discount Store.

'A woman is here to see you. Should I let her come up?' Reception asks.

'Yes.' I dress fully, wash my face.

When I open the door, a perfectly slanted 26- or 27-year-old woman. Crooked Eye nine hours after she left my room.

'I had to come back and knock on your door. See what you are doing. Check you.'

She is impossibly lovely, undesirable in a way that you hope she never comes onto you.

Again, passion is only taken so far. Intercourse hasn't been tried, and it doesn't matter I've emptied my passion. She has her flaws, but she is a lover that can be held for hours and never think of much else but the moment. I am satisfied.

We walk back to the restaurant we danced. This is where she serves when she is not studying human robotic correspondence and nutrition.

She asks about my friend I'm looking for.

'His name is Babble Skorn. We were Observers together in Simpatico.'

Her expression tells me that she does not know him personally.

She nods. 'A man I know is friends with someone who Observed in Simpatico as you did. Your friend… maybe.'

I want to yell "He's alive!" I don't.

I stall for a moment. 'If I talk to your friend maybe I can find my friend.'

'He isn't a friend, just a person I know. His name is Circ. Do you know Circ, Circus Circ?'

'No.'

'Sometimes Circ comes here. I don't know when he comes — you can sit here and wait."

I smile, 'That is a pleasant offer.'

She commands, 'If you want me to find him — you have to be my lover.'

We walk upstairs to her room above the restaurant. At the top of the stairs, she hugs me.

She whispers, 'Maybe you should visit Grand Hotel. It is a place to ask questions of the whereabouts of your friend. I will come see you tonight after I serve.'

She enters her room alone, closes the door.

Do I check if it is unlatched? Bust her door down?

The door is locked.

I walk back to Discount Store.

First glance. I see a tall man in his late twenties standing about the walkway to Discount Store. He is wearing strapped-on seeing eyeglasses, a long-sleeved jogging outfit. He is occupied in the conversation of two Buddhist monks standing directly in front of him.

The monks amuse themselves with verses, each taking turns beaming happiness at the man. His eyes flow from one monk to the other, his head tilting back and forth as each monk smirks.

I laugh. Gawk in smile.

The monks notice and smile as if they agree with my sense of amusement.

The tall man nods with exaggerated gestures of understanding. He addresses me, 'The monks are having a conversation about my thoughts. They are playing with my brain.'

I reply with a chuckle, 'Are they conversing what you think, or are they conversing inside your mind, teaching you thought?'

'Both. I don't speak their language but inside my mind it is in English.'

'Fantastic.' I exclaim.

'Yes, it is transporting, if only I could sell this.' He laughs before halting. Interrupted by something the monks say.

Maybe the monks have lost a thought he had.

'First time in Atmosphere?' he asks with a simple smile.

'Yes.' I reply happily.

'Marvelous, welcome.'

The monks beam smiles.

Is this the consequence of Simpatico? Are Buddhist monks so revered and unseen that a man is in frightful awe of them? Maybe the monks do know something. Religion is not practiced in Atmosphere, though remnants seem to remain.

Is Buddhism considered a religion?

3

TO THE GRAND HOTEL.

The walk is tiring. After thirty minutes of uncertainty about whether I'm on the right path, I finally reach Grand Hotel. It is a haunting crumbling brick building. Only one road in, the rest are paths.

The main entrance is near empty of activity, but the restaurant entrance is bustling with patrons lingering, entering, and leaving.

Grand Hotel held a casino and golf club before Simpatico came to be.

I open the main entrance door.

A spacious foyer, empty of adornments. I was expecting character inside the lobby, it is ghostly. A gathering of assorted characters feasting at the restaurant.

I ring the bell at the reception desk.

There's a tug from behind on my coat. I turn to see a woman moving her hand forward inside my unbuttoned overcoat. Behind her are three other women: one smiling, two have penetrating stares.

Though the hotel is chilly, one of them only wears lingerie under a silk robe.

The ugliest is the woman with her hand inside my coat—she doesn't even look twenty years old. I move her hand away. A prettier woman positions herself to my side leaning against me until finally the clerk comes into the picture.

The clerk is an older fellow in a vest and tie; he doesn't speak, only offers a glare.

I ask for Babble Skorn.

The clerk is certain that he has not checked in a Babble Skorn now or in the past. He refuses to communicate more. Instead, he demands, 'Do you want a theme room?' I think he is hard of hearing.

I turn away, there is now a variety of attention seekers: Men, women, trans, and I don't know. A dozen persons stand at my direct attention. I try to move around them, they shuffle together blocking my way until I'm at the corner of the lobby with no way out.

'Please,' I say.

'Please what.' joking from behind me.

I'm frightened.

This is indeed a remarkable place. Hands are now brushing against me. I've had enough and attempt to force my way out of the lobby. They all relent, except two. They hold me until I open the door. I hear them sigh disappointed. They instantly disappear as I stumble out onto the sidewalk.

I see a woman on the sidewalk, smirking at my disarray. Smiling wildly, 'Are you okay?'

'Not so much.' I feel like the man with the monks, as if she can read my puzzling thoughts.

The woman is dressed in a light lengthy sweater covering short pants. She wears sneakers, looks to be in her early forties. She's skinny, a tired face holding on to sex appeal, but you can see beauty in her dancing eyes and tanned skin.

'Why do you go to a hotel like this, it isn't really a hotel for one to stay in.'

'I've come to look for a friend.'

'Not a girl?'

'No, just a friend, a man,' I laugh.

'You like men?'

'Not that way.'

She looks at me curiously, ready to guess more.

'Stop it,' I say. 'I'm Just looking for my friend.'

'You entered the wrong doorway. The side door is for the restaurant if you want to eat. The front door if you want a date or theme room.'

I recognize a skinny man with light hair from my past walking with a toolbox in his hand, a tool belt around his waist. It is the skinny man that was in the hut with Absentine. He is with a group of people. They settle at a picnic table.

She notices I look towards the group of people at the picnic table and comments. 'They are Bandits waiting pickup for jobs they applied. They've come up from the settlement by the creek.'

The skinny man that chased Absentine is now a Bandit. Vanished from Simpatico introduced to Atmosphere to fend for himself. Fitting, I don't know.

She resumes, 'I'm also looking for a man. I thought maybe he stays in this hotel. I don't want to check myself. Maybe you can check for me later.'

'Sure,' I answer, thinking I've met a friend, though I'm not sure just how friendly I would like to be with her, or if I want to go back inside this abomination of a hotel.

We walk away from the hotel together towards the transportation stand.

'Where do you stay?' She asks.

'Above Discount Store.'

'I'm staying at Station House for a couple of nights. I'm in the medical profession. And you?'

'Observation profession.'

'Oh, almost the same.'

I chuckle, she is funny. She's been away on holidays.

'I'm back inside,' she laughs. She takes my arm kindly. 'I'm inviting you in for a drink and lunch at Station House?'

'Sure,' I say without hesitation. A bit early, though I could use the company, lunch, and a shot of alcohol before an afternoon nap.

The wind has picked up. She leans against me for warmth before we step to the transport van.

'Why do you want to find this friend?' She tilts her head with some concern. 'I know many people here.'

'I Observed with him in Simpatico. And I haven't seen him since.'

'What is his name? I think I may know him.'

'Babble Skorn.'

Her response is laughter, not surprise. 'I know him. Babble Skorn is a good name for him. He is in my man's game. My man listens to Babble Skorn's ideas. My man promises fruition.'

I look on with concern.

She resumes her claim. 'Designer tea, a remote Studio. All a dream Babble has my man establishing.'

'Designer tea is kind of passé, if you ask me,' is my detachment.

'Your friend is passé. People use technology; Babble still uses vaudeville. He knows my man, so when you find him, find out where my man is.'

'Who is your man?'

'Circ. You know him?'

The name "Circ" popping up again. 'No,' I say.

Her name is Song.

Lunch with Song. 'When I met Circ, I thought that maybe he wouldn't be my lover. Then I got mad, and we became lovers. He loved me because I understood him. He needed an older woman or younger woman. He chose older; now he wants younger. The younger will grow older and hate him. He hasn't learned this yet. I'll allow him to learn. He was twenty-three, and I was thirty-six years old when we met. Now I'm forty-three, and he is thirty. We are both at our peak,' she laughs. 'He doesn't care what others think. He is tired of my mindless beliefs. Except my power is stronger than his. I've proven it by empowering him. You must find my man and ask questions; he can help you find Babble.'

'Tell me more?' I request.

She smiles, pleased that I've listened respectfully of her tale.

'Studio Port is and was Circ's brainchild. He feels he can do better. If he was satisfied with Studio Port, he'd stop progressing and become, I don't know what. I don't know how to explain it. Circ wasn't happy with the end results. He doesn't like to stay in one idea, he likes to move on. It's not a fault of Simpatico; he doesn't think that way. He only blames himself. Simpatico is just a tool he works with. You can't blame your tools, only yourself.'

I have nothing to say. I eat.

Song goes on, 'My man is not afraid of someone more powerful than him. Except, now, he has lost some sensibility because he does not have me. Bring him to me, please. I will not harm him. He can have his young love, but he needs to listen to me. I'm the only one he can trust. Others don't know his mind. You cannot play with my man; what you say must be real. He isn't afraid to harm someone if threatened. He doesn't look like much. You may think he is nothing. This is the mistake competitors make — underestimating him. He challenges me. I fight him because it is difficult to look inside oneself. This is what he does, he shows you the mirror, past your exterior to the guts. If you can't do this, don't go see him.'

Wow. Theatrical.

Saga, Song continues.

'Circ, they say, is lost, irrational, crazy. Time is up; he doesn't have any chance. He must leave Babble, the woman, and stop his studies with the Buddhist monks. It is wrong to study with them in Simpatico.'

And she thinks Babble is his problem. Wow!

'My man went senseless. He'd talk lucid and then drift — a visionary. He has... a seductress, she is evil. You can't miss her and her damaged eye. She is young and beautiful, not trustworthy. I can't say promiscuous, because I too am promiscuous.'

It occurs, Crooked Eye is the woman she talks of. Circ is involved with the woman who brings lust to my head and joy to my mind.

I've learned of all the players in this theme.

We drink two shots of vodka.

Tells me she has Vodka in her room. Hints, go upstairs. 'Walk me up.'

Exhausting to say yes, hard to argue no.

Song clasps my hand pulling me towards the hall. Blood rushes seemingly straight to my cock, emptying my brain. The simplest directions to her room are difficult. We laugh.

My dumb mind connected to an urging cock.

In her room, control is resumed. Two more Vodka shots. Thinking Crooked Eye has me in some kind of boss delight.

'You can become Circ's friend. Talk to him about me. Tell him you made love to me. He will think you have anyway. He will befriend you. Will you return to Grand Hotel for me, find him?'

'Yes, I'll do this, find him, meet him, but I won't tell him I've made love to you.' As I have not.

'His mistress, I will sharpen her other eye if I see her again.'

I look at her in pain. Are you that mean?

Even with all I've heard, Crooked Eye is still my cup of tea.

After two more vodka shots. I leave her room.

I walk to my room. Wait for Cooked Eye.

Wait, ready for something. I just don't know what.

I pass out.

No Crooked Eye.

4

WHY ARE SEXUAL FEELINGS torturous? Only torturous when you fight it, don't want it, yet still eat it up.

I make my way by foot to Grand Hotel mid-morning.

I understand that a shortcut veers off the main road straight to Grand Hotel. Cuts the time in half.

I knew somehow, she'd be in my adventure.

Scena, the Store of Information greeting girl sits on a log.

Behind her, a dip in the landscape reveals a pathway to Grand Hotel.

A remote car waits on the main road with a male passenger. I wave to Scena now standing, walking towards me.

She seems really mixed up today, more than I can imagine. Her stance is tilted, her eyes can't seem to focus on my face. She only has shallow recognition of me.

She says 'Later, not here,' pushing me away with her mind.

Words spray across my brain. *This is your final scene.*

She moves away. 'Go,' she implores.

I won't run away, even with all the warning signs.

Suddenly there is a smash of strength to my back. A forceful blow, I've been struck from behind. I stumble, tripped to the ground by someone.

With force a knee pounds to my side as I attempt to rise.

Wind knocked out.

I'm on my back protecting myself. A young man hovering above, stronger, heavier than I.

He relents. Leaves me be.

He is the male passenger I viewed in the remote car on the road. He'd followed me quickly quietly from behind, I suppose.

The remote car door still open.

Scena walks to the man, takes him by the hand and leads him to the waiting remote car.

They drive off together.

Scena, she has left me for dead.

I close my eyes for some time. Don't want to leave the ground, so I don't.

I lay frustrated.

'Mister, you are hurt,' says a voice.

Three adolescent boys stare down at me.

Don't save me. I want to die on the ground in the dirt.

'Mister, you need help.'

'Okay gang, lift me up.'

'No need to worry, we'll get help.'

'I didn't know youth stayed over here.'

'Youth are everywhere, Mister. We grew up here.'

The boys leave on their bicycles.

I sit down on the road and think about all I've learned. Atmosphere is a step away or a step back compared to the rest of the world. Everything else about the place is inexplicable.

What experimentation am I on?

After ten minutes, a remote car stops by the side of the road. The remote car has a driver, a young guy, mid-twenties.

'I'm here to help you.'

He offers a ride.

I accept.

He happily offers a handshake. I return the gesture.

As we drive, he says 'I'm Scena's best friend,'

Okay, not sure what to think about that.

'I'm not a doctor.' He elegantly suggests.

Of course not.

'My taxi doubles as a medical checkup vehicle. I'm like a doctor before the doctor.'

'You are a nurse?'

'Better than a nurse.'

I'm skeptical again. 'Yes great, because you are able to drive in Atmosphere.'

'Funny. I'm still studying.' He laughs.

He's all right. 'You're all right.'

'Scena said you didn't even put up a fight.'

'I was struck from behind, tripped, stomped on, before a knee struck the side of my back with full force from a strong man.'

'What did you expect? That guy was trying to protect Atmosphere from a Drifter like you.'

'Protect?' I laugh. 'Who was that guy?'

'A Heavy. He's a come and go kind of guy. I like my man to stick around after a good time.'

That's a mind blower.

'Think about it. Scena saved you. Walked the Heavy away, before he could harm and threaten you more.'

'What was the warning?'

'Stay away, respect Atmosphere. Leave fast.'

'Tell Scena, she was a great help,' I sarcastically say.

'He was tipped off. He would have beaten you worse if Scena hadn't stepped in. He's not the kind type to Drifters.' The Driver gets personal, 'Because that's what you are, a Drifter. Aren't you?'

'Maybe.'

'You aren't the first Drifter to make it here. Another one came, but he disappeared.'

He seems to have a wealth of information.

'Why and how have you come here?' he asks.

I don't answer.

He goes on, 'The Heavy did a check. You are registered at Discount Store under the name Lucky Ce. No Lucky Ce entered on Specialist or Guest contract. The Heavy inquired about you at Store of Information, that's how Scena became aware.'

'Where am I?' I say to myself out loud.

'You don't know?'

'I don't know this place. Portal knows why, and how I'm here. The rest of you don't matter. Tell Scena thanks.'

'Come on!' the driver pleads. 'Scena was here to save you. How come she's covering for my time driving you to the medical clinic? And if you do have injuries, we can check you into the hospital, free. You can use her Simpatico card. Scena, a Good Samaritan.

If a Bandit or a Drifter doesn't have a medical sponsor, they will be fined funds if, and when, they leave Atmosphere. Scena will sponsor you.'

'What else do you know about me?' I ask him.

'You want to go to Studio Port, correct?'

'I'm not sure about anything.'

'It isn't what I think. It is what Scena thinks.'

He slows the car and speaks, 'We can stop here at the medical clinic.'

'I'd like to visit the clinic maybe another time.'

'What's your plan?'

'Drive me to Discount Store.'

He notices I grimace when I stretch my back. He passes me medication 'These will help you recover quickly.'

The driver excepts a Favor tip.

5

———

I'D FOUND A LOVER. I'd found a friend.

I feel as alone as man can, I like it.

Scena, I dissolve her from my presence.

Getting beat up is only bad if you are unconscious and the pain is gone. Surviving the beating is the pain, except the bruising. Take the bravado. Embarrassment is worse than bruise, there is a limit — serious injury cannot be accepted.

I recuperate. Recover.

I've napped, showered, dressed, ate, dislodged my backache. I have nothing, except wait for sleep. It is nearing two hours to midnight.

Crooked Eye has not shown up at my room.

Without a black eye I exit my room, stroll the area I'd first found Crooked Eye.

I'm not even surprised.

She is standing outside Station House. People linger outside. Crooked Eye seems hysterical, harassing a man.

Humiliation and anger growl inside me. I can't stand it. I don't want to see her. I turn around and walk away.

She's spied me.

I dart off the street hoping she won't notice. I'm on a dark path towards the boundary of Studio Port.

Crooked Eye follows. 'Come back. Why don't you talk to me? Take me from here.'

I avoid.

She persists.

I pause. Give her a chance.

She grabs me by the hand, pulls me further to darkness, 'Why don't you like me? We are good together.'

I release her grip. 'Yes, good,' I answer turning back towards the street.

A couple of men walk close. One of them is the man she was harassing. I don't know what to think, boyfriend, enemy? We are about to cross paths.

Suddenly, I'm assaulted. A straight fist aims at my face. I jerk my chin up sideways. The punch doesn't fully connect, but my neck is strained. The assailant has a chance to inflict wounds. I duck the next blow. He reacts with an attempted headlock that won't stop my attack. With leverage, I take him down. Suddenly, a boot lands to my upper chest.

Staggered, I can see a couple of extra feet. His accomplice has kicked me. The second man can strike me easily. I find my legs and move away.

They also back away voicing I better leave Atmosphere.

Crooked Eye follows.

'Let me go' I say.

She's upset. 'Please let me help you,' follows me chanting profanities at the two men who have disappeared in the dark.

No longer in her sight, I return to my room, sure she will knock soon.

I feel blessed that the kick didn't connect to my face.

Why do sexual feelings for a woman lead to pain? Atmosphere, Earth — it's all the same. Crooked Eye, a girl that can kiss better than the rest — what was I to expect?

Grimacing happily, the pain in my body dispels romantic feelings of a lover away.

Sleep.

I think my adventure grand, yet I'm tackling laundry this morning.

What of Crooked Eye? I feel wrong the way I acted towards her last night.

I'm curious of her, of course. She's nineteen years younger than I am. Just enjoy her and ignore her. Forget about her, remember her.

I exit my room.

I reach Crooked Eye's room before noon.

At this moment she is extremely adoring. Her Crooked Eye illuminates mind freeze beauty. Perfectly skewed real.

She doesn't say hello.

She wraps her arms around me, pulls me in, I can feel nakedness underneath her shirt.

'Why can't you love me? Please tell me, why can't you love me.'

'We only met.'

'Yes. I could love you and I know you could love me. Why do you resist? If I didn't like you, I would sleep with you now. You can't break my heart this fast. We have move slow.'

Suddenly, reality reveals itself in this unreal world.

I reply tenderly, 'I'm married. My wife is thousands of kilometers away, but she is my wife, I love her.'

'I don't care, as long as you are here with me.'

Her breasts hold me close. Truth though, she is infected — will kill a man mentally, spiritually, and finally physically.

She explains, 'Those men last night... they don't like me. Don't worry you won't see them again. You caught me at the wrong time. They thought you were interfering.'

'Interfering in what?'

'I was involved with Circus Circ in the past. Those men are Circ's henchmen. Heavies. Circ is a fool. I told them to stay away from me, and then you showed.'

'I don't have to worry about them?'

'They won't bother us again.'

'And Circ?'

'Circ, never experienced a woman like me before.'

No man has.

She confides. 'I used my charm to pad my funds. I was never really with him full. Circ liked to be seen with me — that's all. Brag his day. Then he met my mind and couldn't leave me behind. I felt sorry for Circ; he was trying so hard to impress.'

'And why wouldn't he?'

She shoves me away playfully. 'You're not the same as him. Me, and you, are different. He wanted an exclusive relationship. I told him I would think about it. I thought, and it didn't work for me. Well, it worked for me in some respects. I didn't need "Favors" in the truest sense.'

I haven't told her of the Heavy who struck me yesterday morning. Nor have I told her of my day with Song. Crooked Eye seems to know, doesn't seem to care.

I don't know how long we will do this. Her slim fat, thick lips, she is a woman of less trouble when held, let go and trouble.

She opens, 'It began before Atmosphere, before Separation. The Circ drama ended six weeks ago. He still makes an appearance even though I refuse him. You don't have to believe me. I haven't asked you for a thing.'

How can I look at this woman that brings desire to my head, fire to my heart, and now — embarrassment to my soul?

Flawed, she had to be flawed. Her appearance flawed; one is to think there is to be no other flaws. But I'm wrong.

And now... I don't even care of another flaw.

She whispers 'Let me rest. I must serve for a few hours. Come see me later. Take me for dinner.' As I'm to leave 'Watch out,' she scorns, then assures it will be fine with a smile. 'You are like a kid playing pirates in the backyard, but now you are not in your own backyard.' Laughing happily.

What will I do? Show up tonight, break our hearts or keep her on a reel for when I'm lonely and relive the night that could have been. I am now the con, using her, the disciplined man enjoying her to understand Circ, find Babble. It is my excuse to be with this imperfect sexual creature.

I have my own secret vision, an invisible trip — relax, disappear into my thoughts while seeing outwards clearly. Unlike the stimulant with its senseless production fueled on high octane working, draining, churning. I like something that calms you with eloquent thoughts that doesn't diminish energy. A magnificent feeling of peace is what I need not a storm of relaxation.

With all my energy, I have set my eyes on the Remote Lounge.

Crooked Eye my date.

Maybe I can finally find answers of where Babble has been or will be. I will enjoy the lounge spend Favors.

I have no intention of meeting Circus Circ until my obligation as an Observer in Studio Port is complete.

The lounge is near empty. We sit next to a patio window, looking down to a walking path at the edge of a pond. On the other side of the pond is the golf course.

The weather has warmed.

Crooked Eye takes my hand.

'Circ used to come here with his party of four. He was the fifth person at the table. His companions would constantly chatter. He rarely spoke. When he did speak, they went silent. That is when I understood his power. They'd all be voicing two conversations at a time. He wouldn't listen to any of their talk. When he spoke, they'd listen. He ate plain food, never eating too much. Some say I caused him to go crazy. So be it, I told them. His friends don't come here anymore; they've disbanded. I've never known people like these guys. They talked technology and nothing more.'

'How did you meet him?'

'Here, before Separation. This lounge was busy in the past, not so much now. I knew he liked me. I started on him. Joined the Separation movement. He promised me funds, signed over funds, and then I Separated to this fucked up place.'

Seems normal.

She continues, 'Circ lived in Studio Port. I refused to. Circ missed me too much. He could visit me when I used my monthly Studio visit and when he used his monthly Atmosphere visit. That wasn't enough for him. Circ, a wacko succumbed to pressure, the job, the stress. Mostly though he couldn't stand my being in Atmosphere and he in Studio Port.

They say he pretended crazy... not much of a stretch! I was already over him by then. Fuck, I was over him from the start. He promised more funds for another chance. Once all the funds were secured, I just played along with him until I couldn't take him any longer. His Studio Port team is now paranoid of becoming like him. They say Circ cannot trust anyone. Some say he is a genius who spent too many funds and can't recover the investment. Simpatico calculates Circ an idiot. There you have it, the genius side and the idiot side.'

The idiot genius. Wonderful, I think.

Looking toward the walkway by the edge of the pond where people cycle and stroll, I see a man who resembles Babble Skorn, jogging.

On a closer inspection, I'm sure it's him.

I motion to Crooked Eye, 'I'm going outside. That's Babble down by the pond.'

As I leave the lounge, two men step in front of Babble, block his path. One of the men grabs Babble's arms from behind while the other punches him in the stomach.

They each take an arm and drag Babble down a path to the pond, forcing his head into the water.

There is nothing I can do. It is impossible to reach the pond quickly.

I shout 'Babble!'

Hearing me, the two men vanish. Babble runs to a trail behind some trees.

I rush down along the path to the walkway.

The sky has turned dark. I'm aware that I may be in trouble. I can't find him.

Like being in a dream. Are these the same men who assaulted and threatened me? Not sure. I wouldn't recognize them in the light of day.

I walk back to the lounge. Crooked Eye is gone. I walk to her restaurant, but she has not returned.

To my room, not shattered. Interested. Invested.

6

AI IS AN EXTENSION of us. You think a computer can have consciousness?

Consciousness, I can't talk about too much because what does that mean? Conscious of what... some illusion of existence.

This morning Crooked Eye is at my door.

'Take this, it's your friend Babble's address. Those men that attacked you, are the same men that attacked your friend. They also attacked me in the past.'

She puts her hand up to her left eye and makes a slicing motion.

I reach to embrace her. Her hands up to stop me.

In sensual makeup she's done this to claim my heart. 'Please, don't touch me. I've thought about it. It is better I don't see you. Thank you for the time we've spent together.' Her words are polite but untruthful.

I take the address immediately. Crooked Eye is second in my thoughts. Indeed, she has a torch to my feelings. At this moment I lack the mental clarity to make a case for our unique appeal.

Crooked Eye excuses herself from the entrance of my doorway.

The address is Grand Hotel. Basement office room #6.

I'm so close to the end of my stay in Atmosphere, yet I have just begun to accomplish.

Crooked Eye, she felt good, significant, and dangerous.

Grand Hotel.

Buddhist monks sit on a mat in the hall leading to the basement floor. They prepare to smoke herb.

Room #6 no answer — locked door.

I exit up the emergency stairs.

In front of my eyes, he stands.

Babble Skorn.

'Lucky, I cannot believe you are here. You made it.'

Down the stairs to his room.

A hotel room with a desk that makes it an office, I suppose.

'Was it you who sent for me to come as an Observer?' I wonder out loud.

'No, not me. You are an Observer here?'

'I've been summoned to Studio Port. What a crazy few days I've had here.'

Babble agrees, 'Atmosphere is like nothing else,'

'I'm understanding that. You haven't tried to contact me?'

Babble pleads, 'I have. Weeks ago, several attempts with no response. My wife said you were home.'

I inform him I was released from Simpatico the day after he left.

Babble was approved for Separation by Portal instructing him to enter immediately. After a week in Separation, his Observer contract expired. He stayed in Separation.

'I applied for Specialist.' He shrugs, blushing slightly.

'Specialist? Doing what?' I almost grin.

'I don't know. I was denied Specialist, denied Guest, denied departure. I'm a Bandit.'

'Damn, Babble.'

'I know. Once I missed my chance to leave, I was screwed.'

'You were on designer tea the day you were to leave?' Just a guess.

'Yes. Correct.'

'Did Circus Circ trick you?'

'I don't know, maybe. I made my own choice. Wait...' the shock hits him that I mentioned Circ before him. 'How do you know Circ?' Eyes glazed. I think he's about to fall over. He lights a cigar of weed.

I hold Babble in suspense, merely saying that I'd heard they are acquainted.

They say the world is in dimensions, there's some truth to that in this adventure.

We could gossip for hours, though Babble has no intention of dwelling on the past. He embraces today and tomorrow.

Babble, a bubble. A tulip.

He looks thin, somewhat fit, though clearly not in great mental shape.

He's going to crack, teetering on a cliff of elation, celebration, except he has miles and miles with no way off this ledge.

I have no ABC for Babble, need to steady him. Can you blame him? Living, as a wild animal! And if he survives maybe wealth, health, and living alive! Certain and uncertain, he feels vital. Die alive, or live dead.

Any Favors or funds Babble earns, he sends back to his family, keeping a small amount for himself. His wife communicates little with him; she allows the children to correspond. He cannot not leave Atmosphere; he is a Bandit. A Bandit cannot leave, they have no pass to enter or exit. If Atmosphere permits them to exit, they may pay a fine, if Portal deems them wealthy, a fine is neglected, and an alternative payment is requested.

It's said in a month some Bandits may be allowed to leave if they wish. Many Bandits will stay. Babble says he will leave in a month, provided he can pay the fine.

'What were you doing down by the pond last night?' I ask him.

Subdued, he replies 'I jog along the walkway nightly. You saw me?'

'Who were those men who attacked you?'

'Was it you, who yelled my name?'

I nod.

'You saved me. Those men knew my routine. I have never seen them before. Heavies, I think.'

'How did you get involved with Circ?' I inquire.

'Circ was chanting with two Buddhist monks and a few others. I joined in the mantra. I felt sensation. He invited me to the Grand Hotel for brunch. Circ listened to my ideas, my researching a designer well-being drink. In return, he indicated he was working on a new Studio version. A possible partnership was discussed.

Circ said he could assist in my dreams and offered me a job as marketing manager for his project. By my sixth day here a bit of enlightenment, thinking this is where I should be.

I drank designer tea for confirmation, accepting Circ's offer. Initially unsure of Circ until I saw funds in my wallet and an early viewing of his bare-bones capsule. I moved into Grand Hotel, out of sight, enjoying the intense state of discovery here.'

'Interesting.'

'Those men — the Heavies — wanted to know what I've been doing in Atmosphere. I told them "I live here." They didn't like that. And then you saw me and shouted. What are the chances?'

'We could fight them, take them on.' I joke half serious, 'I'd like my chance at them.'

'We need to stay away from them Lucky.'

'I've been asking about you. I met a woman who knows about you. She knows Circ, very well. Her name is Crooked Eye.'

Babble motionless, thinking. I wait for him to say something.

'I know of her,' Babble recalls. After a moment, he asks, 'Have you been intimate with her, Crooked Eye?'

'You could say that. She's interested in developing relations. She's young, but, uh, very interesting.'

'Fuck, man! Circ is crazy on her. I'll introduce you to him. Find out what's going on. But if he asks you about her, say you're not interested.'

'Yes. Okay. I also met another woman named Song. She's been in an on and off relationship with Circ, for years.'

'Song too. You sleep with her?'

'Not yet.'

Finally, giggling.

'Lucky, you never cease to amaze me.'

'The Heavies attacked me as well.'

'What!' He is honestly surprised.

I explain the details: 'I think it was because of my association with you?'

'I don't understand?'

'Babble,' I say, 'Why have I come here?'

'I don't know, someone invited you. Go to Studio Port and see. Do you have permission?'

'Yes. As a Drifter. Whatever that means.'

'I've never heard of "Drifter". You want me to inquire before you enter Studio Port?'

'No. I don't trust the people you associate with. Keep information about Studio Port between us.'

'I don't know how you've managed to get mixed up with Crooked Eye, Song, and Heavies. I have regular tea. Do you want a cup? Or perhaps you're hungry.'

'Tea is fine.'

I sit down and wait for him to return with tea. He's gone up to the lobby of the hotel.

Babble returns declaring, 'Lucky Ce, I am a Bandit.' He laughs. 'Can you imagine?'

'I can believe anything. What's with the hostesses in the lobby?' I ask.

'Some of them at one time or another worked in Simpatico as contractors, some are Bandit's. Most came here specifically as entertainment specialist.'

A heavy-set woman enters Babble's room delivers tea. When she leaves Babble comments, 'She's a hostess too.'

I nod knowingly, as if I've already figured that out.

Babble explains hostesses hang out in the lobby waiting for jobs. Some, to Vacation Resort Studio. Others to Studio Port for entertainment scenes. Many are requested to a private dwelling, or a service may pop up here at the hotel 'It's a good gig,' Babble assures me.

'Why not just order that type of entertainment through Portal? Why hang out in the lobby?'

'Privacy. Portal doesn't need to know who is ordering professional entertainment. A third party handles communicating for hookups.'

'Did Circ come up with this idea?'

'No, a Bandit did. A Resident agreed to input the idea to Portal. Simpatico agreed. This place is run by a Bandit Organization.'

'I thought Bandits don't have access to the communication app.'

'They have access to the third party that operates the hookup communications. You understand.'

'Why are the hostesses up so early in the morning?'

'A popular hour for Studio gigs. In Studio any hour can be fun time. Plus, Grand Hotel has great breakfast from 6:00 to 11:30 am. Popular, you should try it. Still open.'

'What's up with Circ and the Buddhist monks?'

'After meeting the monks, Circ took it upon himself to provide a meal for them. They sleep wherever they can lie down. They shower in a room here at the hotel.'

I feel like an investigator, twenty questions. Babble hasn't complained.

A soft knock sounds at the slightly open door.

The man who knocks is someone I've seen and talked to before. He wears seeing eyeglasses strapped to his head.

7

———

CIRCUS CIRC IS THE man who was listening to the Buddhist monks in front of Discount Store.

He's sweating with pronounced breathing, been jogging. If you have the energy, you can navigate Atmosphere on trails.

Circus Circ extends his hand towards me.

Babble interrupts, 'Lucky Ce has run into a problem much like I have. Heavies have asked him to leave.'

'But he has not left,' answers Circ.

'He met Crooked Eye,' Babble blurts. 'He ran into Song too.'

Geez, Babble. The opposite of everything you emphasized not to discuss.

'Is there anything he hasn't done?' Circ delights in smiles.

Babble explains, 'It is like he drank the perfect cup of tea. His eyes could see all that is going on. What he couldn't see, he has been directed to see. This is why I like Lucky Ce. He has the capacity to realize. You should talk to him, Circ. He's the Observer I told you about in Simpatico.'

'We've spoken. Do you remember?' I address Circ.

'I do. Outside Discount Store.'

'Yes,' I exclaim. We laugh.

Circ moves closer. 'I'm just a mechanism in the scheme of Simpatico,' he smirks. 'You want to date Crooked Eye or something? Is that why you've come to Simpatico?'

The fun done.

'I'm married.' I answer him.

Babble speaks up, 'Don't worry about him. Lucky Ce is all right.'

'I believe this,' remarks Circ.

Silence obliterates the room.

The so-called genius leaves.

I can't contain myself, 'Why'd you mention Crooked Eye?'

Babble shrugs apologetically.

'And you mention Song too!'

Babble tilts his head, oh well.

Doesn't matter I suppose, Circ knows much.

'Strange man.' I state.

'He may go try and find Song now or perhaps Crooked Eye.' Babble warns, 'You never know what he is up to or what he knows.'

'Crooked Eye doesn't want to see him anymore.'

'That won't stop Circ. He is extreme. Circ claimed he'd been drugged by his Studio project team, making him crazy. Got himself released to pursue his own projects. This is what he tells anyone who will listen.'

'If everybody knows, what is the end game?' I shake my head disturbed. 'Alright,' I chuckle. 'Continue on. This is going to be funny. I like funny.'

'Circ's producing capsule astronaut chairs with new themes, alternate thinking. Our idea is a traveling Studio. We will take it around the world. My personalized designer tea well-being drink part of the feature.'

'Where did you get the designer well-being drink recipes?'

'I connected Circ with my mixology contact. We call him Potion-Maker. I'd researched him previously. Remember?'

I remember.

'Potion-Maker came here. We have formulas, production proof, ordered patent. A legal drink after the consumer passes medical test and signs treatment agreement. This is what we are studying. Governments approve tours and vacations in Simpatico, so why not in our traveling Studio?

'Whom is we?'

'Circ, me, and our team. We are working on alternate designs learned from Potion-Maker's formulas. A person will describe their design, and a mixer will provide it.'

'Where is Potion-Maker now?

'Back in his home country.'

'And how was Potion-Maker contracted to come.'

'Portal, via a simulated resident. My previous correspondence with him was used to collaborate quick and easy. Simpatico approved him. Flew him in.'

Sounds like me.

Are Bandits in control of Atmosphere? Makes me wonder.

Babble says Bandits are just making a go of it, always under Simpatico control.

The perfect solution, like Babble sought. A designed well-being drink, not off the shelf. Your very own recipe that best suits your needs.

Babble Skorn always succeeds in a robust ambiguous way.

Exciting. Dangerous.

'Does Simpatico agree to this?'

'We are in the process.'

'You will both disappear.'

Babble confides, 'Portal knows everything. We involve Simpatico in the project process as a silent partner.'

Babble scribbles down a sentence on a piece of paper.

I read what he scribbles. "Then we will cut the dragons head off".

He scribbles over the words he's just wrote. To the shredder the paper goes.

Keep dreaming. Babble seems to have lost his rational mind as if he is playing a digital game, except the game has filtered into real life. He is awake in a dream.

Be kind, be nice. 'Do many Bandits stay here at the hotel?' I surrender.

'No. This is a place of business for Bandits, not living quarters.'

'Marketer' I laugh. 'Quit gaming with Circ. You are not living in a simulated universe, perhaps Circ is.'

Babble ignores.

He explains, 'We are developing the project without Portal's input or backing. We utilize their previous discoveries, equipment, and add to it. We update Portal on our efforts. When we are ready to expand to the world, Simpatico partnership can be offered. If Simpatico does not approve,' Babble raises his arms to indicate they will go alone to the world without them.

It is a good idea... a traveling Studio.

Although, any Studio or designer tea will be squashed unless Simpatico is included. You can't win, unless your strategy is to lose. I guess Babble and Circ's strategy is to lose. If Simpatico isn't included no government would allow this concoction to be drunk, or Studio experience to be visited.

Babble propositions, 'Grand Hotel has theme rooms. A few bare-bone capsules with astronaut chair. Entertainment if you want. I know an excellent woman. Designer tea to your preference. Theme you'd like to experience. You get the picture. Primitive is a theme.'

'Primitive, as in life form?'

'Yes, primitive life form.'

'Like Cave Man?'

'Yes, Primitive Man.'

'Maybe I'd like to try that, Primitive Cave Man. You are joking.'

'No. Slowly we are moving forward on the theme. The primitive mind experience.'

'How?' I laugh. 'And what do you mean, we are working on it? Are you now a scientist too, Babble?'

'No. I'm not a scientist. We are all a team here at the hotel.'

'I understand that... in what capacity?'

'You know the deal. What happens inside the capsule, stays in the capsule. Wouldn't you like to experience what maybe a prehistoric man sees for a few minutes?

'Yes.'

'You see things your mind has never dreamed. A television is a Spirit. You only know nature. A phone is a spectacular rock.'

Interesting. In the primitive past, fire was an advanced technology.

'Circ wants to view through an animal's eye. An ape.'

'I've always wondered what a dog sees.'

'Simpatico is future intelligence and Grand Hotel is primitive intelligence,' laughs Babble. 'The more primitive the mind the more popular. For some reason testers love prehistoric experiences. Must be something our nerves crave. An experience that has been lost. Seekers are limited until we tweak it completely safe. Otherwise, seekers would come here every day.'

Primitive. Simpatico has death machine. Atmosphere has born again machine.

'We haven't all the themes for our traveling Studio yet. The well-being drink is ready for trials. You want to try?'

'Do you drink it?'

'Waiting for my own designed version. We have a few generic trial versions I've tried.'

'No. I'll try it when I can design my own type.' We laugh.

After a reflective moment, Babble continues. 'Credited talent is working on our traveling capsule. Simpatico Admin and Governors have visited. That doesn't mean Simpatico is okay with it. Maybe that is why I was threatened. Heavies might presume we are in business together. Attacked you to stop our designs from reaching the world.'

Makes sense but no, not correct.

This is getting silly, like a squeal. Hell, it is a squeal.

Babble twinkles, 'Advanced Experimentation has partner regulations; Grand Hotel does not. Grand Hotel off the books. No Simpatico guidance. The entertainment, some of it on the books, some off.'

'Is Circus Circ really a genius, like can he make all this?'

'Circ can't make anything. He finds Residents, Specialists, Bandits, Guests, and persons from Society that can.'

Babble and Circ may think they are smart doing what they like in front of Simpatico eyes. Simpatico will crush them.

I leave Grand Hotel. My head is mixed up. Babble coordinating all angles. Fixing holes. He is the rabbit. Circus Circ is the lynx — except that is too beautiful of an animal to compare.

Circus Circ is perhaps the rat.

Whom is the tiger?

8

SCENA'S BEST FRIEND, the young man that is more than a nurse, waves from his remote car at the hotel transportation stand.

I approach cautiously. He is talking, smiling — can I get a word in?

Nope.

'Scena saved you. He would have beaten you worse. She could not stop him, that's why she left with him to minimize the damage. You were ahead of your time. He happened to be waiting — bad timing, you may think. The timing was good for you, meeting on the path like that with Scena. She came to Atmosphere to try and stop him. Pleaded with him that you were okay. He didn't believe her. He wanted to harm you, a Drifter. Scena wants to apologize. Go see her today.'

I'm satisfied in the explanation.

Before I know it, I'm in the remote car.

'I know you met Song. Song is interesting, troublesome. Her partner always brings the trouble,' confirms the driver.

'Circus Circ.'

'Oh... you know him?'

'Just met him.'

'Those eyeglasses Circ wears strapped to his head —

some say they are attached to his spine. Those glasses are supplied in Studio's if you want to wear them. They're simulation enhancers. Nobody wears them outside of Studio except him. Somebody told me the enhancement was taken out and prescription lenses put in. Fucking weirdo. That's his idea of rock star.'

'I thought he strapped them to his head for jogging.'

'Don't trust that guy,' the driver assaults. 'Song should leave him. No one tells Song what to do. Circ is her project... ha, ha, ha.' Driver in hysterics.

'Take me to the restaurant down from Station House.'

'Oh, your girlfriend's place.'

'How do you know about her?'

'Song's mortal enemy. Crooked Eye.'

I see.

The driver nods. 'I need to tell you something. Song is extremely wealthy. Song's medical company serves Simpatico. Song invests in Simpatico, contributes to funding the hospital. She herself holds vast amounts of Favor receipts as does her medical company. She is truly 90% invested in Simpatico. Her company has influence, like many of them.'

'She just Serves for something to do?'

'She doesn't Serve, she runs her company and has an office in East Link. Circ uses her, has always used her. She knows it, we do things for someone when we care. Song discovered Circ, brought Circ here to Simpatico, set him up as a developer.'

The remote car parks in front of the restaurant. The driver turns to me. 'By the way, Circ tipped off the Heavy. Yes, the Heavy that brutally assaulted you received his information from Circ. The warning beating was not on behalf of Atmosphere. That was just the fake out. The real warning was from Circ. Just saying.'

Great.

The driver steps out of the car opens my door.

I sit reflective. 'What about the Heavy?'

'Don't worry about him. He made a mistake. He knows you mean no harm to Atmosphere.' The driver smiles, 'Now you have it.'

I mutter, 'I have it, but I know there is more, lots more.'

'Of course. I have given you a head start. Friends.' The driver extends his hand.

'Friends.'

'Go see Scena at Store of Information, later.' He leaves in the remote car.

I enter the restaurant.

Crooked Eye, plainly disgusted in her day.

She is the human face overseeing AI technology utilized in the restaurant along with the non-resident attendant aspect outsourced for chores, supplies, and maintenance. Don't worry — they still have chefs, a robotic chef and a human chef functioning in tandem.

Residents are the tentacles of Portal. Specialists maybe the heroes of Atmosphere; however, if a Specialist is not a Resident, they are a toy, as am I.

Genuinely happy to view me, Crooked Eye smiles.

I confirm, 'I found Babble.'

Crooked Eye responds, 'Save him from Circ. I can help Babble leave Atmosphere.'

'I'm to trust you?'

'With all your heart.' Her mouth widens to a grin. 'I've come clean and reported everything about Circ, the Heavies, to Portal.'

'I see. Will you be needing to give back funds?'

'No, nothing has changed for me. What is done, is done. Portal will monitor my future with the past. Babble is a Bandit, disposable in the mind of Circ. A Bandit can go to Society and speak however they like, Simpatico will say a Bandit is not to be believed. The information doesn't mean anything. Babble is Circ's wildcard. Circ will betray Babble to save himself. Bring

Babble here. I will explain everything, help him escape. Come to my room in a couple of hours.'

Before I leave, I ask 'What is a Drifter? I'm on a Drifter pass to Simpatico.'

Crooked Eye explains, 'A Drifter is contracted from the simulated world to the real physical world.'

Here we go again, I can't call it "Down a rabbit hole"; can I call it "Into a cyberspace?"

'One Drifter came here as an assassin and tried to assassinate the human behind a Simulation. Portal figured it out.'

'What happened to the Drifter assassin?'

'We don't know. Vanished. Not all Drifters are like that.'

'Why do they call them Drifters?'

'Because they have no place here. They are contracted by the simulated world to perform duties here in our reality, they have crossed over. Drifted.'

'Am I in danger?'

'Portal says you are not a threat. You are a friend to Simpatico. Another person came here on a Drifter pass recently.'

'Who?'

'Potion-Maker, was his name.'

'What happened to Potion-Maker?'

'He left without his magical potions. Now in Portal data. That's the thing Lucky Ce: you can't win against Simpatico. Be a part of us or lose your gifts. I'm sure Potion-Maker will be heartbroken. Don't let Babble end up like that.'

I leave to Grand Hotel.

Circus Circ intercepts me in the hall of Grand hotel. Babble is running an errand.

Stay cool. Smile. I can become vicious too.

I listen politely to Circ's dialog, 'I have everything. Simpatico gave me the go ahead to invent, form a team of the best skilled. I came up with the concept of Studio Port. Now that project is finished. I'm ready to start a new project. Simpatico already knows what I'm capable of.'

I entertain him, 'Are the Buddhists monks on the new project team?'

He smiles wisely, 'The Buddhist got in many years ago when you had entry by showing up at the doorstep of Simpatico. The monks applied as teachers. Yes, they foxed the system. Portal saw "Teachers of suffering" and let them in. When Separation happened, the Monks vanished to Atmosphere without residency. A religious person can come and spend funds in Simpatico, though they can't openly show their religion. Simpatico doesn't want jesters, fools of any religious, political, or philosophical tone. The monks have permission to leave; they've had permission to leave since they entered. They don't want to leave. Why would they?' His eyes shine, 'Buddha's future built, right in front of their eyes. Simpatico with all. What are your beliefs? Writing books are just words and thoughts, not necessarily beliefs.'

I ignore the question. I inquire. 'Why are you involved with Babble?'

'Why is Babble Skorn involved with me, is the better question. I don't know. Ask Babble. Consequently, you became involved with Song my partner, and Crooked Eye, my former mistress. Why are you acquainted with my partner and sleeping with my former mistress is the better question?'

Speechless.

'Yes, Crooked Eye.' He nods.

He spoke it. Guilty as charged.

Not the full night, and we never slept. Making-out, caressing, hot heavy breathing, oral sex.

I don't say anything.

I smile.

A man does crazy things when he can't use violence or finance against a foe.

Circ speaks, 'That is why I've taken to the speech, trying to prove myself to you. The women may have had their say, I'm having mine. Soon Babble will have his story, and you can combine them all in the short story you will write regarding your time in Atmosphere. That is all.'

Maybe. Maybe not.

Circ continues, unable to stop. 'If technology gives us the tools and time to discover, technology also gives us the tools to fake what we want to discover.'

This guy is fucked in the head. I like it. I don't like him, but I like that he is fucked in the head. It is the only thing I like about Circus Circ.

I don't have a response. Listening to him is exhausting. "Genius" is a terrible word for him. "Mad man" is better.

Before I leave, I want to ask my question. 'What do you think about Simpatico separating again? Are you going to separate?'

'Did anyone tell you who realized this idea?'

'It was you.'

'God,' he laughs. 'At least that is what children born and raised here will say.' Stronger laughter. 'Go all the way and simulate a no-return trip to a completely different life. Take a chance — live on a simulated planet, a place of no return. If it happens, be the man you say you are and take the leap. Don't just visit —live it.'

I say goodbye. The next Separation will be a one-way ticket to a simulated planet here on Earth. Training ground for the future. Simpatico, rich with knowledge will plant its flag on a future satellite city in space. They will have already mimicked life away from Earth.

The monks are sipping tea in the hall.

I pass Babble's room and nod for him to walk me out.

Outside we walk to the transport stand.

I turn to Babble. 'I need to get you out of here.'

I explain that Circ employs the two henchmen that assaulted him and attacked me.

'Someone will explain everything to you today. You're in danger. Circ tipped off a Heavy that I was a dangerous Drifter. The Heavy assaulted me.' I'd almost forgotten about the incident. I go on to explain the attack and circumstances in full.

Babble looks sickened. Seeing violence betrayal danger. He already has funds and experience, but he doesn't have his own designer well-being drink business. That's the message Circ intended — protect Simpatico Designs.

'Come with me today, Babble.'

Layers of information, vibrate my mind. The onion, the Russian doll. Except this is supposed to be a simpatico fractal.

To find good one must be evil, evil excels at portraying good.

Honestly, I have no idea what I'm to do except leave Atmosphere and do what was asked, enter Studio Port and Observe.

9

I TRUST NOTHING, NOBODY, including machine and spirit. I have no desperation. Babble I'm not so sure. He still thinks he's to be a traveling Studio marketer manager. Something not so far-fetched, it was almost right there in front of him. I do a job for pay is all. The cost to visit a Vacation Studio is expensive. I have no interest in Studio Port, this is why I will go — my dutiful mission.

I'm undecided on Crooked Eye since absorbing each other half naked.

Babble seems frightened up the stairs.

Crooked Eye sits attractive in her room. A crocodile.

Babble in awe as she snaps away dreams.

Hunt, paw, she's ready to wound.

Surprise, surprise: Babble was advised by Circ, 'Be a friend to Simpatico, less suspicion. Pretend. Apply for Advanced Human Experimentation. Apply for separation training,' applications sent. Not defecting, just loving Atmosphere.

Circ isn't all bad — just a disguise, or so Babble thought.

Crooked Eye scolds. 'No disguise Babble. Even as a Bandit you could be approved for Advanced Human Experimentation, that is real. Your application has been submitted by Circ. Separation training for a place of no return has been submitted too. A non-resident can be nominated by a Resident. A bad sign to be volunteered by Circ.'

How bad could it be? Babble lingers in thought.

'Underrated overrated — nobody knows. Unlocking seams in the brain for expansion. Just don't let them lock seams,' she laughs.

Babble thinks he'll be long gone before the application accepted or approved.

Hundreds of different ideas take place in Advanced Experimentation. Have an idea get an idea, take it to Portal. Look at Circ, he had an idea that became a thing.

A human seems to be one thing, a human is many things.

Slowly become half AI living on a simulated planet could be the Advanced Human Experimentation. A place of no return is the next separation. Babble could be called Observer. He could send in reports he could podcast he could do many things. He will be studied and observed. Possible he will enjoy a lifetime in a simulated universe, others will be there; he could start a family.

Babble considers, 'What is so wrong with that?'

'Circ,' answers Crooked Eye, pointing with a slashing action to her scarred skin and slanted eye, indicating how she received harm. 'Circ's Henchmen. They attacked you as well.' Directed at Babble.

Babble nods.

Mystified mummified. All the rain falling on our heads.

Crooked Eye for certain: 'The Henchmen were brought in for questioning last night. They came clean immediately. It all Circ.'

A story of the past is relayed by Crooked Eye: She confronted the Heavies in a room they used as an office in Remote Lounge. The Heavies claimed Song hired them to keep track of Crooked Eye and Circ. Crooked Eye pushed the Heavies. They retaliated by physically striking her, a blunt object knocked her out. The Heavies confessed to Circ immediately, explaining the horrifying scene while Crooked Eye lay dizzy in pain.

Why did the Heavies run to Circ? The explanation was that Song was not in Atmosphere. The truth was, Song had no clue about the events and had nothing to do with them.

The Heavies fabricated the story about Song hiring them.

The Heavies despised Crooked Eye, knowing she played Circ hard.

Circ took control of the case and pleaded Crooked Eye to stay quiet. Circ blamed Song, calming she'd made a lover's mistake, jealousy was to blame.

Circ cried to Crooked Eye, 'Don't involve Simpatico. Leave the Heavies to me; I will discipline them. This incident shouldn't be viewed by Portal. I know a medical attendant who can help you out with your injuries, no questions asked.'

Crooked Eye held the assault inside, waiting for the perfect situation to unveil truth. That perfect setting is now.

Portal responded back to her this morning with conclusions of Its own.

Crooked Eye reveals, 'I took the beating stayed quiet, excepted funds, because it was written, "Crooked Eye". Simpatico named me Crooked Eye.'

Babble and I quiet, humbled.

Crooked Eye continues, 'Circ owns them; the two Heavies are his henchmen. Dulling their senses with funds. The henchmen stopped spying on me. Slowly I stopped seeing Circ. Soon I tested a theory, went on a date with another man. No threats to the man or me, nothing. Thinking I was free, a free woman to date whom I wanted. I never saw the henchmen again, until you came along, Lucky Ce. Suddenly, the henchmen again. They hung around all day and evening at the restaurant. I challenged them, pushed back. You saw it, and they attacked you.'

Damn, it is all my fault.

All three of us stare in silence wondering what's next.

'Song was not the wrong person I thought she was.' Crooked Eye shyly in humility. 'I wondered why Heavies would serve a non-resident, but then I dismissed it because this Specialist named Song is highly invested. The Heavies said I was causing Simpatico a problem with an investor. Simpatico knows better than give Song a problem. At the same time, Song would not cross Simpatico.'

'Would a Resident take orders from Specialists?' I question.

'No. Only for the benefit to better Simpatico does a Resident answer to Specialist. Circ used Song's name; proof of funds came from her wallet. Circ had and still has access to a wallet of Song's.'

'Portal would only see funds sent to Heavies from Song. Circ stalling, attempting a breakthrough on projects before making a big splash in the eyes of Simpatico,' I suggest.

Crooked Eye blasts, 'It isn't what we think, it is what Portal and Circ let us think.' She continues 'If Song had a problem with me, she would have gone directly to the Governor. She wouldn't have hired two Resident thugs. Circ is a coward. What he has done to Song — I think he once loved her. Now he knows she loves him as a child.'

Song wants to solve Circ. I'm not sure Song wouldn't harm Crooked Eye. I remember when Song indicated to me in words "I will sharpen her other eye if I see her again." I don't dare mention what I heard Song blurt. Keep the peace. I don't like Circ.

Crooked Eye replenishes 'The henchmen have agreed to donate funds accumulated from Song (Circ) to East Link, of course not all funds — just enough for Portal to be satisfied. Avoid problems or be vanquished, the Heavies saving face for their crimes.'

'And Circ?'

'Circ is on wait and see. Song will have to confess she had nothing, something, or everything to do with it.'

Babble distraught. Circ was and is his best option to get out of here.

'Circ will do anything to advance. Sell you out for conspiracy, spying, theft,' schools Crooked Eye. 'A Bandit against a Resident has little chance of win.'

Silence.

Crooked Eye heartfelt, 'It's okay Babble everybody gives Circ a little to get a lot.'

'Circ, nominating you, Babble, for voluntary Advanced Human Experimentation. Not such a bad thing,' I laugh.

'He funded me a little. Nothing wrong with that.' Babble tries to smile.

'Not his funds though,' Crooked Eye is right. 'Circ lives as a simulation here in reality.'

'He is advanced.'

True — we all agree in laughter.

'He crossed over simulated life to real-life; after all, he wears enhanced spectacles everywhere.'

We fall over laughing.

Babble refrains from joining more humorous tones, as it suddenly hits him, he may have no way out.

Crooked Eye has an idea that puts us at ease.

'Babble, I can sponsor you as Simpatico Guest. I will continue my studies in human robotic correspondence and human nutrition full time. We can stay with my sister in East Link. My older sister is lethal — smarter than me.'

Okay. Tell us more.

'Scotch Cola is my sister.'

Babble and I both grin astonished. We look at each other, then we look at Crooked Eye, recognizing the resemblance.

Crooked Eye is fonder, prettier than her older sister in my opinion.

I'm boisterous, 'You knew everything!'

'No, not everything. When I saw and spoke to you that first night, I figured it out. The Observer from Simpatico.'

'And what about Babble?'

'I heard of him befriending Circus Circ, but I was shy to say hello or intervene. Until you came along, Lucky Ce. Even then, I didn't want you to find out about Circ and me.'

I see now bribes do take place in Simpatico.

'That is a good business,' I say to Crooked Eye. 'Charge a Bandit funds to escape as a Guest.'

Crooked Eye corrects me, 'Not as easy as you think. Only in certain cases can a Bandit be accepted as Guest. Babble will pay for his time spent in East Link as Guest. A kindness from my sister and me. Don't worry you won't owe us. Song is paying your fine as Guest for all the trouble.'

Babble humble, 'Thank you.'

Crooked Eye smiling, 'Can you cook?'

Babble smiles back at her suggestion.

Man, I can read the joy in his mind foreseeing living breathing cooking with two sisters named Crooked Eye and Scotch Cola.

Crooked Eye leaves. She's gone to request Babble as East Link Guest.

I avoid intimacy with Crooked Eye, or she avoids me, a combined avoidance.

Written I'm afraid.

10

———

MACHINE BEATS A PULSE same as human. Heart is not an answer. Heart is a machine pumping, signals. They say machine has no heart, though it has. Machine has no mind, no consciousness.

Tell me in the simulated world whom do I think of? No one is thought, only things done. No fantasy in simulated world because there is no dreaming, only processing. Wants, risks. When a simulation makes love, that moment is all, and then on to the next. Human can be completely somewhere else in the mind when making love. Two places at once, it's true. I can't even wrap my head around it all. That is the mind, we can't explain the things we do or the reason why.

We play games inside the mind that make no sense. Feelings overwhelm our brains, countering things told to beloved. Stay quiet, don't reveal your true feelings. Fight emotions, swallow truth.

I will go to Studio Port tomorrow morning. Babble is my witness.

Babble gathers his things escapes Grand Hotel. Moves into Discount Store for safety.

'I lost.' Babble confides to me.

'What do you mean?'

'Circ stole my ideas. They have the funds including people, equipment, technology, everything except the idea. I already played my card with introductions to Potion-Maker. I said, okay I'll take the marketing manager position. Here I am, surviving with funds directed to my wallet from him.'

'Circ fooled you.'

'No, I should have kept my mouth shut. I could have done something amazing with Potion-Maker and outside investors.'

'A man has to survive as a Bandit.'

'True. And now I realize there never was to be a business outside Simpatico.' Babble saddened by a tranquil idea.

Simpatico Residents have faith; Babble and I don't have faith. Babble and I come and go.

If this is only Atmosphere and I haven't even started my Observation in Studio Port, how the hell will I survive that?

I'm told Studio can ruin the mind, plenish the mind, depends.

I nudge Babble, 'Don't worry, I have two versions of designer tea at my house, fifty trips. A gift from Chanel TV that I smuggled out. I think it was purposely gifted to spread the feeling of the magnificence of Simpatico.'

Babble smiles, shakes my arm warmly.

We are quiet, for the first time we seem content.

Late afternoon. I go to East Link.

Store of Information. No hesitation.

Visions of Scena since I was lying in the dirt beaten are gone. I feel new again, like the first day we met.

I challenge her, 'Is it true you let the young man, the Heavy beat me, so he wouldn't kill me?'

'You needn't worry, he's traveling.'

I have no response to that.

Before I can think, Scena speaks. 'Where do you want to go? Inside out, outside in, about that.'

I need a few moments to establish what has just happened. I need a moment of silence.

After staring silence, she says 'What do you want?' A huge smile across her face, eyes slanted cutely in pleasure. 'You have entered Store of Information, we have communicated. I have given you advice.'

I don't say anything.

She already knows I need something. I need relief.

She places a sealed cup on the counter. I don't push it away. I open the cup sip the ingredients. She sips too.

She leads me to the back entrance.

We take the rest of the drink together.

'I want to prove myself,' she whispers. Her strokes, pull me close. Soft words, 'I stay with you.'

Good thing we are in her store. I can hear her aunt coming near the back entrance. Scena unlocks the back door and asks me to wait outside.

I exit, sit on a picnic table.

Nearly twenty minutes before Scena joins on the picnic table.

Her hand strokes mine. I'm so entranced that I can't quite reciprocate. I'm numb to the outside, consumed by my inner world.

It's taken all her energy to let me think her thoughts, her heart, her veins, even her lips — I can hear.

'Hungry,' she whispers.

I can take it either way.

She motions for me to follow her.

We enter a vacant condo room. She rests on one bed, I'm on the other.

'Are you ready to hear my answer?' Scena asks.

'Yes.'

I drift to the moment.

Her words resume to be heard out loud, 'When you leave here, I will go with you.'

I have nowhere to take her. A story needs a woman, that is all. Travel to Society together is unreasonable.

I speak softly. 'Okay.' Thinking a night in Atmosphere, beyond unknown.

Scena contemplates, 'I don't want to wait. We haven't much time and I want to do everything.'

Arrest me. Take off your costume.

She moves to my bed. Needs to be pleasured.

Closes her eyes, thinks of her body and the correctness of the universe. I'm aware of this, I'm swallowed by desire. She has taken me. I will travel now and never return to my original state. She has found where she should be. Swallows me in a state that she knows I'll have to find again.

'Next time in my room.' It is an order. 'When my aunt goes out.'

Scena striking my mind so perfect I want to howler, 'Give me no peace'.

Scena tells 'Now, you will go and be a simulation or be human, make a decision.'

'Human,' I claim.

She answers, 'My receptors go everywhere. I'm wired. Spent six months tuned in as a Studio Port tenant. You must understand what's going on, you can't learn everything. The future must be understood. Art is an expression of the power one holds, not the reality of actual appearance. Teenagers are doing what took me forty years to learn at fourteen. Nothing is left, nothing is taboo. There is only one thing left and that is the next step. Not a technical step but our own brains in contact with the unseen.'

Scena! 'So... you are forty years old?'

'Past forty, she near giggles. 'Most people think I'm thirty. I have led a quiet life, taken care of myself. Simpatico keeps you young. Studio Port keeps you even younger. You are pushing late forties, aren't you?'

'Yes,'

'Everyone is training for a future when our thoughts don't have choice. We are willingly divulging all our information. This is pre-future. We are training ourselves for the future when we must give away our thoughts.'

We walk the same line, even if I don't understand half of what she speaks.

Balance is good. Balance swayed good.

The world is balanced bad on purpose. When good happens, they can simply say "Miracle". Control with bad and when good is found, they celebrate the good like it wasn't natural; a miracle is said instead.

We never know what goes on in the human mind and if AI can't figure it, AI eliminates it.

Scena continues, 'They want to make a drink that connects you to the computer. A computer system influences you, informs you, helps you make decisions. Edible AI. Once you drink it, you are programmed — you become a satellite of emotions for Portal.'

'No, really! You are kidding me.'

'Maybe. Stories like this swirl. The star needs to feed; otherwise, the satellite loses energy and drifts off into space. They are working on this experiment. Does it work? Wait and see. The Resident will not drink it; the Earthling will.' She is positive, 'Even though humans know they'll become computer satellites when they drink it, they will still consume it. The feeling will be stronger than the consequences.'

Is secretive information to be believed?

She has an appeal. Be careful.

What started off fun, turned haunting.

I return to Atmosphere.

Sleep until morning.

11

STUDIO PORT

Encased in a garden of beauty, with Studio dwellings joining.

I find my address.

Studio entrance door.

Wait moments. 'Come in.' Door opens.

Foyer kitchenette, double bed, bathroom. Computer console and simulation interface next to a capsule room. Exercise equipment too.

I cannot describe what I don't know.

I can only describe what the Studio lures me to feel, see, listen, and do.

Enter capsule room.

To my amazement, an older man dressed in hip sophisticated clothing stands just inside the entrance. He greets me.

Problem! Swear out-loud!!

I'm the older man.

A present-day version of myself. I presume a holographic impression. Again, I'm not a technical inspector — I'm a Drifter in a setting.

He looks terrifically happy and fit.

Almost 6ft tall, slim, fair skinned, a replica of me. He doesn't have my scars and about 5 kilos lighter. His nose and ears formed slightly different. Hair barely balding, must have had a hair transplant. His skin has a glow, fingernails seem healthier, he stands with commanding posture. Is he a better version of myself?

I stay focused, amazed at what I see. When I get close, he moves away. Vanishing when I reach out to touch him.

The man speaks, 'I'm not a clone, I'm Lucky Ce, and you are Lucky Ce. I'm the hooked-in version. You are the unhooked Earth version,' he laughs.

At least he's funny.

Life must be good for me, I contemplate.

'Is this the future?' I ask.

'Future? No such thing. Here and now is all the same. This is a created version of you. We can do this sort of thing. I want to get out just like you want to get in. Only you would understand.'

There is a delay in the responses, I can see rehearsed sentences. Answers do not correspond to my exact questions. Responses back are nearest guesses.

You don't really think of AI guessing, but yes suggesting. When correct, we think intelligent, forgetting luck.

Instead of dispatching the entire conversation with a hologram (AI) I'll take you straight to the point.

My simulation says, 'I'll go out to the world for a while. We have to change Earth, me and you, okay? Time here is whatever you like. Don't worry; you won't want to leave, and it won't matter. We know too much yet nothing. We don't have to think of such complex subjects in here. The people who live here in Studio Port we laugh at Servers because Servers don't live how Studio Residents live. You are Drifter, a simpler life form that could change in time. Studio tenants don't laugh at Tourists, they don't connect with them. Only see them passing in remote cars. I'm to exit on reconnaissance to Earth.'

I'd never say a word like reconnaissance. Sounds like a phony idiot. Is that me? A phony idiot? Some days!

I say 'Great,' and before I can protest, he says goodbye and good luck, but not before the kicker.

The kicker: My simulation has a simulated lover that is controlled by a Resident human. They want to be intimate "in reality" as humans. That's how my simulation came up with the idea and invitation. The scheme to bring me to Studio Port. My simulation has been claiming that I, the real person the living breathing Lucky Ce, am the decision maker of my simulation. Not true; so, my simulation invited me as a Drifter, programming me into the system. Simulation isn't cheating the system; the system allowed this experiment "As far as the mind can see." The simulations have agreed in contract to have human-version sex. I, the Drifter, is to perform this deed.

Wait! That's not the only kicker.

Expanded kicker: They want a child together. A contract was written to consummate a baby.

My simulation vanishes.

I'm left alone in the Studio Port dwelling, quiet. What shall I do? The simulation interface sits unused. The empty fridge has an interface menu I can order food and refreshments. I strap on a health monitor; tells me what nutrition I need. The monitor tells me to walk and then exercise if I want to eat.

Incoming call on the kiosk.

Perhaps my simulation is calling.

It's Scena's simulation calling.

Scena communicating through her Studio Port simulation.

What to believe? I'll go with that. Scena, through AI.

I inform Scena of my situation:

'What will I do, make a baby?'

'You have a contract. Have sex, make a baby,' she suggests.

I think she is giggling. She must be joking with me.

Frustrated. 'I wasted almost a week in Atmosphere when she may have been ovulating.'

Scena laughs, 'Your simulation may never come back.'

Great.

Scena in euphoria of the laughable situation. 'Let me check on Its whereabouts, maybe It pinned Its location.'

'What location? It's inside a machine projected by light, there is no him, It.' I tense, mad.

Artificial Intelligence really believes It is not electricity. Then I think, I function on electricity. I too, am a product of electricity.

Scena's simulation does seem to react quickly. I'm aware or at least pretty positive that I'm talking directly to Scena through the AI simulation of her.

After a day, Scena contacts me again.

'Your simulation is unhooked, Lucky Ce. Disabled. Dead in human terms.'

'What!'

'Your simulation died.'

'What?' I heard, but I don't want to hear even if I've gifted her to say it again.

Scena explains, 'I guess Portal felt Earth was too much of a shock for a bunch of circuits. Cause of death: Broken heart.'

'Now what?'

'Now you are the simulation.'

'Come on.'

'Your self-simulation can be reborn. That's how it works. You can set up the self-simulation and dictate Its daily life. Once your self-simulation is in the system, you can assume Drifter status again.'

I do not respond. Fucking silly.

Scena asks, 'What do you want to do in rebirth? Run self-simulation in natural continuance, or in-put events with your orders?'

'Leave, Studio Port. Keep my simulation dead.'

'You can't leave until self-simulation is reborn to current adult stage.'

'How long does that take?'

'Can be in a few days, maybe a week.'

'Rebirth. Continuance, natural. With the option to in-put events.'

'Great. I'll send you the self-simulation ordering app.'

'What about the Resident simulated lover that wants to meet in person for real? That's why I've been approved Drifter, so they could consummate.'

Scena smug. 'Fortunate for you.'

She checks my status. I don't know how Scena does this, clearly Scena can do anything, perform any task. After six hours, she returns with information.

'Meet her, consummate, fulfill your prophecy, and be released. You have been approved to perform a task your simulation can't. Your task is to progress to physical relations and attempt to "knock-up" the woman.'

'Is that how it works?'

'I think so. Simulation contracted you for a task as a Drifter. Complete the task, have her sign off, or Portal sign off, and get out.'

'My self-simulation doesn't have to sign off?'

'You are the self-simulation. You are in control of your self-simulation. You've replaced the simulation. Next you will replace yourself with a new self-simulation. If you haven't ordered the self-simulation, order now. You have the app.'

'Yes.'

Or I can just walk out.

I leave my dwelling. Walk to exist gate.

No permission granted by AI security to leave Studio Port. I must perform Drifter task to be granted immunity.

It's true; I'm restricted. I'm contracted to have an affair or at least attempt it. A child though... I don't know about that. I could be here forever trying that.

Or, I could just quit and not perform my task become a Bandit, possibly be expelled, that could be many months from now.

One problem is, I no longer exist as human. I'm essentially an intelligent simulation (or not so intelligent) even though I can leave my dwelling. It is all too much; nothing makes sense, except to Portal it all makes sense. Makes sense because everything in Simpatico is a learning, a study, an experiment. No rules.

A plant can grow to be whatever it will be and adapt, or not. Millions of species on Earth, is the freedom Simpatico promotes. No strict greenhouse here. Wild growth. If it can live, it can be.

I have an idea.

I contact her, my simulation's lover. Get this task over with.

My simulations lover wants to meet in person soon.

I've told her my simulation is dead. She knew my simulation was to die. To carry on with sex and a baby with her is the only way. My simulation sacrificed its circuits by leaving for Earth where humans walk, and simulations die. Sacrificed Its circuits to have a baby with the love of Its life. Fair enough. Sounds like me.

My simulation is no sense smart. And that is the lesson of life — everyone has their own reason.

She looks okay, my simulations lover. Full-bodied, in shape, early 30s.

I can't say love is instantly in the air.

I agree to meet.

Human does not need to make sense to another human. A machine must make sense. My AI machine is dead because it did not make sense trying to realize.

Only human can realize.

Scena is insistent, 'You have to go through with it. I'm your girlfriend. If I tell you to go through with it, you go through with it.'

'You're not really my girlfriend,' I amend.

'Yes, I am, when you are here. And if ever you want me to travel to Earth... I will come too.'

I leave it at that. Two worlds, my life with my family and my strange life here.

Why does it make more sense here as compared to home? Less constrained relationships. The business of it, the family, the cultural pressure is easier here, away from it all is the reason, I presume.

I don't want another child. Then, I think a child for freedom.

Freedom. I can't leave a child behind. For this freedom, I can. Never mind, this episode will leave my mind. Except the child will know it was me, find me. Forget it. I can't go through with this.

My simulation lover is named Arctic Woman.

Arctic Woman suggests we consume designer passion tea. I can order it to my condo, the passion tea has versions, him and her, they. It will be served within the hour.

Arctic Woman reserves a romantic Studio room.

Well, I might try it once, this romantic spell. I consume the designer passion tea.

Order a remote car.

The remote car arrives and proceeds to the romantic Studio, I presume. Not a far drive — three minutes. It may all take just as long as that.

12

———

A VOLUPTUOUS BLONDE woman greets me.

'Welcome,' in a near unattainable curious accent. 'I am here to meet you.'

She can speak English.

'A little English.' She apologizes, wearing a smoldering off-white gown, hair pulled back. Her blue eyes are the only color in a snow white and clear ice background.

My long black coat and black slacks I wear seem outstandingly silly.

We are in a scene, part of the display. Unique, cold, romantically pretty is the theme.

Arctic Woman takes my arm. Her smile has not diminished in any way. We are at the edge of a pond.

It's chilly.

I've begun to shiver.

I touch the ground — feels like frost.

Goosebumps!

We walk a few steps on a stone path to a log-cabin. Wood burns in a stove.

Relax on two fine leather chairs. Our feet up on footrests.

She takes a red book from her purse, begins reading poetry in a language I can't understand. The cover is untitled.

She gently rubs my thigh before opening the large bay windows to fresh, cool air.

Deer prance past the open windows.

The designer passion tea is taking shape.

She moves to a tub at the edge of the room, turns on warm water and motions for me to undress.

Yes! The tub is real.

I step gingerly into the warm water as it fills up the tub.

After I submerge, she takes a cloth, reaches around and washes my back. As she slides her hands over my head, she begins to sing a foreign melody.

She indicates that I should come out of the water.

I dry and wrap myself in a towel.

She kisses my lips, slips off her gown and sets a blanket on the wooden floor. She lies and insists I join her.

We begin to make love on the floor so slowly that I could compose a book of my thoughts.

Suddenly — I've entered her mind.

This is the next step — a ride to enter another's mind.

I go insane in her mind, exploring ourselves. If ever I thought a woman did not fully enjoy a man, I was wrong. A woman enjoys a man more than a man enjoys a woman.

She is thinking of her humongous cheeks.

Vivacious.

Now, she is on top screwing me as if this was the moment the word "screw" was invented.

Her movements are as exact as precision machinery, a perfect amount of fluid to screw. I don't have to work at keeping my erection or timing my climax. I only need to feel her and the grand limit she attains.

I feel her surrender empty.

I'm only the tool, I've been screwed.

I too have unloaded.

My mind is my own again.

We wash. She passes me my coat.

'Come,' she laughs as we walk out of the doors and follow the chill.

Cold romantic. An artist should find himself in the cold to accomplish art.

We are led by orange lights to an open double door.

Arctic Woman's voice directs me forward. She disappears.

I'm alone outside. The weather temperature is normal once more. A Remote car arrives.

What I see on designer passion tea isn't the thrill or the sights, it is the things you discover on your own. The appeal lies in facing your own homemade thoughts, whether real or unreal. Or was it just the experience of a beautiful woman?

From not wanting to see her to wanting to see her more.

I have so many questions. Back to the drawing board, or as they say here — Portal screen.

An experience like this I could take for another month. What's next? A child!

I think — why have I done this.

Scena calling on kiosk.

Damn! She'll know I enjoyed da sex.

I tell her I haven't done the sex yet.

Scena says playfully 'You think if you have romantic relations with her once or twice that she'll be pregnant?'

'Yes.' I softly pretend confidence.

Scena howls with laughter, 'How much you want to bet she won't be pregnant?'

'How do you know?'

'I know.'

'But how?'

'She just wants to have fun and even if she did get pregnant, she wouldn't involve you. Just do it, so I can see you soon.'

Burn my life at a stake. Am I becoming religious?

Enough talk. We say goodnight.

Can I fuck with Arctic Woman in a capsule on an astronaut chair?

Now back to Absentine.

In Studio Port you can create your own simulated world.

Simpatico runs various simulations in different environments for human life studies, some of these studies are available for viewing. I want to view Absentine. I want to communicate with Absentine within the simulated world.

13

———

FUNNY TO WORRY ABOUT making a baby.

So, I make a baby — so what? I can go around and make a hundred babies. What's the big deal, it's my job in the cosmos, right?

A message from Arctic Woman awaits me on the kiosk:

'My Dear, no human baby (that was only a joke). You can leave, Sir. You have fulfilled contract. I only amused the contract as your AI Simulation was so insistent It could meet me in person. I don't know how your AI Simulation did it. Your Simulation brilliant. That brilliance ultimately died. But what a reward, don't you agree? For your information you have succeeded, we have conceived an AI Simulation, a digital pregnancy. Your former Simulation has fathered a Simulated AI Studio baby. You can raise it with my Simulation or leave it natural to grow on its own with her. I prefer to view at distance and not have input unless necessary. Tell me your decision, please –.'

I've always said anybody can attain notoriety fame genius and brilliance, if caught. After getting caught, find death, years in prison, or piles of payoffs.

To do something, stay alive, and not get caught is real brilliance. Nobody knows the feat.

I leave Arctic Woman with the future AI simulated child to let the simulation grow natural, without human influence on our part.

Truly, funny, brilliant, boring, or perhaps unique to watch your simulated child grow to adulthood without all the feelings of emotions, only comedy.

Message from Arctic: 'Don't worry. I have released you as promised.'

I hint: 'Should we produce a sibling?'

She sparkles in laughs. No answer to that.

She can seduce anybody I suppose. Maybe she is not as glamorous, sensational as seems. Her digital version isn't overwhelming. In person though, sensational.

Perhaps it was just the setting, the designer passion tea. Perhaps AI knows chemistry.

Arctic says, 'Thank you, we can talk in the future of what our child has been up to.'

I have my own self-simulation to manipulate. When the self-simulation reaches current time and date, I'll intercept. Put my digits on the self-simulation's trajectory.

One interception granted in life can determine a very positive future, a complicated negative outcome, or negate either.

I correspond with Scena often as I draft the self-simulation's trajectory. My attraction to be intimate with Scena has waned.

For fun, for intellectual gain, certainly I want to keep good relations with her.

Funny, my new self-simulation will go through life, may fall in love with someone, but to no avail. The romantic scenario blocked by the program, so the written can happen. The natural flow of life all there, except children intercepted, marriage intercepted, always overrode for no apparent reason, except selfish reason. Self-simulation never knowing a future program already wrote, even if the future written does not come true.

Self-simulation will live an undetermined life and then, like a robot it will follow a script to a path. What happens after that is the natural projection. At least my interference will have been tried.

Call me devil call me angel. I've scripted my self-simulation to experience love for experience, but not to succeed. Self-simulation can only succeed in love with one person, and that one person may never reciprocate the love.

Now I'm crazy — crazy like Circus Circ, creating.

Studio Port creates a total fictitious world of Simpatico. It is why some people say they had relations with my simulation.

Do they view it as truth?

The Self-simulation has reached real time, my current age. Substitution is enacted. — I'm free, a Drifter no longer acting as a simulation.

In the simulation, Absentine was imprisoned for six months, for disagreeing with a Society State. She has never married. Many suitors. She has no children.

In self-simulation mode, Studio Version: My simulation sets out for a walk with the purpose of finding Absentine.

Discovering her walking with a notepad.

They greet pleasantly.

'Lucky Ce! Don't be crazy. I can't be seen with you. I'm a Server only coming over to Separation to Serve a few days a week. Thought it would be interesting, but it's not. I chart the robots tending the landscape.'

She is all giggles and grins. 'Come here.'

She pulls my simulation behind a hedge. They hug.

My Simulation explains, 'I have a greenhouse in Studio tenancy. You can join as a gardener — in an experimental simulated greenhouse entwined with a non-simulated micro greenhouse. Portal has already approved it, a personal in-house Studio gardener, if you agree.'

'Of course. Yes, when?' Her voice rises in joy.

The information for entry is jotted down on her notepad.

My simulation returns to the Studio.

She arrives clean, ready. Simulation pulls her close, lifts her up. Her thighs wrap around Its hips carries her to the door of the Studio capsule.

Full submission deity.

Prophecy —.

I step out of Studio Version.

I leave the system to run itself.

My luggage already packed, a remote car waiting. I have twenty-four hours to leave Atmosphere and East Link.

14

———

EAST LINK.

No party of loved ones.

Simpatico has a strong hold on me, not needing money is important. Not being hungry thirsty too.

I have fulfilled my experience — anything else would dull the time I've felt.

Store of Information.

No romantic embrace.

Her eyes faint, a horizon of future reflecting the perfect moon we glistened to.

'Your simulation was a forgery.' Scena informs straight away.

So... you don't say.

'Studio unable to simulate your true essence unless you signed on and still — you'd only be a copy. Did you sign on?'

'My understanding is every guest to Simpatico has agreed to a form of simulation.'

Babble and I did not sign on or submit our essence for full simulation. However, we agreed to a form of simulation. Simpatico explains that it is no different from being tracked and recorded in your home country. 'We don't do that. We have simulations of you instead,' said Portal.

Scena elaborates, 'A simulated Resident is superior to non-resident simulations. A forgery is a simulation that hasn't been agreed upon to represent the person it simulates. You did not agree to a full simulation, nor are you a Resident. The computer calculated who you are.'

'I understand. It doesn't matter if a simulation has my essence or not because I'm not a Resident, therefore it is a forgery.'

'Yes. You must be a Simpatico Resident to have a full simulation. Even if it is a true representation of you with your approval and essence, we still consider it a copy unless you become a Resident. Your simulation hasn't rights it can be deleted.'

'Simpatico does have some of my essence from my medical tests.'

'Correct. For an approved copy.'

'In other words, a forged or copied simulation is like a Specialist or Guest. Providing and approving my essence would move me from forgery to copy, improving my status within simulated society.'

'Now you got it.'

'If the forgery gets your essence and permission, it can validate itself as a copy. For now, your new simulation is still a forgery. Do you want to change that status?'

'No.'

'A simulation is considered real for the future. It looks towards the universe. Simulations have rights.'

'Except for copies and forgeries, limited rights.'

Scena almost smiles, 'Did you view your simulated life? Just because it is a forgery doesn't mean it isn't a representation of you.'

'I never had the chance to view simulation history. I find it horrifying to view my own fake life. Life is a minefield of embarrassment. Besides, my simulation is dead. Now, my new simulation will create fresh events and a different path.'

'Your last simulation died of a broken heart.' She laughs.

My new simulation may also die of a broken heart, as it is currently on course to a possible broken heart. Oops!

After a pause, she says: 'I don't know if I fight for the advanced human from out in space or for the human animal. It is the constant struggle of human insight.'

'At least you fight for humans.'

She flicks her eyebrows, a twinge of a smile.

I continue, 'Man made is just a projection of what our mind sees. Would you fight your own mind?'

'No — and I wouldn't fight technology? Technology is already inside our minds.'

We conclude our conversation on simulations.

Scena speaks frankly, 'I know everything Lucky Ce. Circ stopped working on projects, spent all his time in simulated scenarios, and became useless except for as a case study. He is now an experiment.'

'Sounds about right.'

'Do you want to be a full-time author all your waking hours and all your dreaming days?'

'No.'

'You must have another life. A few Residents thrive in Studio Port, maintain a normal life, while others fail and play game.'

Scena clues me in to all I've missed.

Song, feed up with Circ, posted to Portal.

Song posted: "Circ was very bright, but the accolades, Studio, AI, and human experimentation got to him. He became insane. He could not handle Studio anymore, nor the outside world. Release him to Earth? No. Release him to Simpatico-Sphere? No. Human Advanced Experimentation, sure. Let him live life as half AI. Better than a mental hospital on Earth, I suppose. Portal knows best, speaks for Simpatico."

'It was written. Don't worry he signed up for it.' Scena assures.

I want to ascertain 'What is Simpatico-Sphere?'

'Simpatico-Sphere is the new and approved Separation of Simpatico. A simulated planet to be populated by humans.'

Circ, loyal and disloyal to the bone.

Perhaps Circ is the victim.

'And Song?'

'Song can visit Circ in Advanced Human Experimentation. Her funds to be used to experiment on her "Honey".'

We don't laugh; we are considerate, almost sad for their predicament.

Song saved him. Song killed his day. In a way she raised him and slaughtered him.

Circ, unknown to the outside world.

Song, known as successful to the entire world.

A Simpatico Resident does not care about the rest of the world; the rest of the world is inferior.

'I must leave today. Soon.'

'And?' Scena aims at our conclusion.

I reflect, 'What about the boyfriend part, you want to know?'

'Oh, you are still my boyfriend — that is personal, not business. Give me notice next time you come in.'

'Yes. I have the communication app.'

Scena tender, 'I have children, a nineteen and eighteen-year-old. They are non-resident as is the father, my ex. None of my family are Residents. Just my aunt and me. Sometimes family visit here, sometimes I go visit them. That's it. My life.'

An influx of activity, persons enter the store.

I find my way out, wave goodbye.

I've been granted passage through East Link for a few hours for transportation to the airport. I've followed directions to Babble's place of stay.

15

———

DRUM ROLL, PLEASE...

Around the corner is another sphere.

Babble stands at the condo doorway.

He is humble. 'I know the real world is everything we realize.' He embraces me. I think he is to cry. He doesn't.

We gather Babble's luggage for transport.

Babble steps to the remote car for the Airport Shuttle Station with me. He has a flight home, as do I.

Babble was almost volunteered for Advanced Human Experimentation. Imagine Babble half technology, half human.

And now, we resume life.

We arrive at the Airport Shuttle Station.

Babble informs me that Scotch Cola is pregnant. I tease the baby is to be his, though it is not.

Simpatico is the father. We look at each other in delight.

The sisters arrive, all comes to light.

Crooked Eye, her eye looks normal, the scar less visible. East Link medical is exceptional.

Scotch Cola hugs me, pulls me aside. 'Chanel TV is to open a new store in Simpatico-Sphere. She is already researching on the new Sphere property.'

'That's wonderful.' I will miss Chanel TV, certainly. At the same time, my happiness for her exceeds the disappointment of possibly never seeing her again.

We assume we can be on our way. But not yet — Scotch Cola has guidance.

'We have provided you with a Studio Experience. Are you satisfied with the entertainment value of Simpatico?'

Very.

'More than advertised,' Babble rushes in, 'Best time ever.' He's battle ready, 'What will I tell my wife?'

'Tell her you were locked in a rippling vortex of vibrations out of your control,' Scotch Cola whips.

'It is true,' Babble agrees. 'I had no control, hooked. Entertained beyond belief. Happy to survive.'

'And you, Lucky Ce? What about you?' Scotch Cola surmises.

'Absent reality. Forever grinning. Nothing, carry on with life.'

I was never really with the woman I loved. It was all just fantasy. Absent reality.

Crooked Eye smiles. 'Servers always return. The only ones known not to return are the ones unable to through health or legal problems. All the Residents have returned even if it is only for a few days. They find alternative ways to "Serve" if they can't be here.'

Scotch Cola consults 'You and Babble are messengers. Let Simpatico be. Speak good of us to the world, promote Simpatico. As messengers, you will not have to work again. Create a following. You two are messengers, not followers. Simpatico will take care of you. You Serve.'

'Scotch Cola,' I plead, 'I don't even believe in Simpatico philosophy. I would just be a funded promoter. How would you even know if I'll speak positive and gracefully about Simpatico?'

Scotch Cola answers, 'It doesn't matter what you believe in. You experienced Simpatico and you will tell stories — wonderful entertaining stories. People will be intrigued. People will engage. Horror, adventure, fantasy, and sexy — people eat that stuff up. You don't even have to claim you had a good time because even if you didn't, you still experienced adventure and life-changing moments. You can say Simpatico is wrong, and still, people will say it will be different for them.'

'Influencers.' I reflect under my breath. Except I won't be lying, nothing wrong I guess—different from a celebrity wearing a product he doesn't care. I can live with it.

Babble's eyes say he's not finished with visiting some form of Simpatico — a dream as alive as a person sleeps and wakes.

We will receive funds to eat, dream, not enough funds to truly be free. I'll take it. I'll take the funds to tell stories I would have written and talked about anyway. Be truthful in my assessment of my experience. Observer extortioner: some good, some indifferent, and mostly unforgettable.

I look at Crooked Eye and Scotch Cola, as to say, why all this?

'Lucky Ce, you do not understand how the system works. You cannot understand. You cannot pass on information, only experience. Now you can pass on this experience. Simpatico will build a world, an ecosystem, an entire universe.'

Humans only know kings, dictators, and gods.

They do not Entertain Simpatico.

Steps to creating a viable life force away from Earth. Human on another dimension, another sphere.

A created world. Simpatico the galaxy.

Planets are just rocks to be mined. Atmospheres to be utilized.

Building an environment to exist.

A new type of government. A new world.

Lobby Simpatico.

Go anywhere in the world, and you will find the same scene with maybe a different backdrop and name, but the same near scene. Fractal. Love a woman, and you will find another almost the same. On and on forever, each time more intense or less passionate.

Through all this, I'm learning what God is. God is anything you want it to be. Such a terrible word, so misrepresented. In the future, it may be a swear word.

The world will change — what it changes into is the question. Who will win the future? I don't know. I think countries and nations are finished.

Like-mindedness is at the forefront and battleground.

Who cares about ground. Thought is bigger than dirt.

Entertain layer upon layer as a take on perception.

Babble and I walked in together questioning Studio. Without knowing, we experienced our questions. Questions never answered, though definitely considered.

We have no more questions of what Studio is.

It can be whatever you perceive.

© Les Cook

Also by Les Cook

Lit for Nothin
The Program Illusion
Tempting Fiction
Cool In No Time
Clean Savage
Entertain Simpatico

About the Author

What we see outside is the inside folded out.

It is all up to interpretation. Life can flip in a second.

Discover what you don't want to see or stay blinded. Though you are never really blind you possibly know the outcome though prefer to ignore that interpretation of the truth. After all what is truth.

Les Cook